---— ⟨ ⟩ ——

GAY EROTIC TALES BUNDLE

Awakening
Submission
Confession
Obedience

Gavin E. Black

---— ⟨ ⟩ ——

This book is a work of fiction. The characters, incidences, and dialog are drawn from the author's imagination and are not to be construed as real. Any resemblance to actual events or persons, living or dead, is entirely coincidental.

Published by Steambath Press (self-published)

Paperback 1st edition published January 2014
Paperback 2nd edition published July 2017
ISBN-13: 978-1927553367
ISBN-10: 1927553369

Awakening

It was my brother's idea to head to the beach. Something I wouldn't have agreed to normally. I hated the beach. Too hot, too sandy, and too damn boring. I would be happier holed up in my room, fucking around on my computer, but he'd insisted, saying I needed to get out of the house. Apparently, my period of moping around after being dumped by my girlfriend, Amy, was over.

"Andrew, do I have to do this?" I asked. "I'd rather stay home."

"I know you'd rather stay home," replied Andrew. "And that's why the guys and I are taking you to the beach."

I rolled my eyes in resignation.

"Hey, Connor," my brother's friend Matt shouted as he banged on the outside of my bedroom window, startling me, then slid into the apartment through it.

"Fucking goon," I said, then shoved him. "Ever heard of a door?"

It was a never-ending playground environment. My brother, Andrew, is four years older than me, chronologically, but mentally, him and his buddies are stuck somewhere in their teenaged years. Me at twenty-two …their behavior was beyond annoying.

"Are we ready to go?" asked Matt as he ruffled my hair.

Fuck that pissed me off when he did that. I wasn't a kid anymore. Yes, I was currently sharing an apartment with my brother, completely rent free, including food, but I was between jobs. It happens to the best of us. Me a little more than others. Being a bartender in a resort town where tourists ebbed and flowed with the seasons, didn't guarantee steady employment.

I smacked Matt's hand away.

"Fuck off, Matt," I said.

"Oh …the princess is touchy this morning," Matt said as he danced around behind me.

They'd never let me forget it. I was five years old at the time, and they'd dressed me up in one of my sister's princess costumes, tiara and all, and taken me door to door to dance for the neighbors. I hadn't thought anything of it at the time. I was a little kid. A little kid that desperately wanted to please his big brother.

When our mom came home from work and found out, she'd freaked out and grounded Andrew for a week. It was then that I realized my brother and his friends were making fun of me. I'd never fully trusted Andrew after that.

"Where's Gary?" Andrew asked.

Matt lifted the beach towel off my bed and swung it at my head, almost knocking me over. Today was going to be all shits and giggles. I could see it now.

"He's in the car," Matt replied. "Let's go."

The ride to the beach was predictably noisy, with the stereo blasting obnoxious, top forties crap, far too loud for the cheap tinny speakers in Gary's car.

I settled into my seat and stared out the window. Amy dumping me had done a real number on me. Not that I'd been in love with her, but we'd known each other since middle school, and I'd assumed she'd always be there. It felt strange without her, as if an arm was missing.

I grunted as a hand clocked the back of my head.

Fucking morons.

"Get out, sleepyhead," Andrew said to me. I hadn't noticed that we'd pulled into the parking lot.

"So, which way to the hot babes?" Matt said as he checked up and down the beach. It was still relatively early, so the sand wasn't crowded yet. We had our pick of decent spots.

"What do you think, buddy?" Gary said to me. "See anything you like?"

"I don't know," I replied and sighed. "Amy and her friends used to park themselves right here near the showers ..."

"For fuck's sake, Connor," Andrew said, shoving me. "Let her go, would you? Amy wasn't right for you. You need to move on."

I lowered my gaze. "I know."

"Let's set up somewhere else," Gary suggested, pointing to where a large group of girls were spreading out their towels. "Over there ...before anyone else claims them."

He elbowed me roughly. "You don't mind, do you?"

I shrugged my shoulders and slung my towel around my neck. My brother and his friends were hot enough to pull in any girls they wanted, and I mean *any* girls, but they were complete assholes to even the nicest of them once they'd picked them up. Miraculously, the girls they ended up with rarely seemed to notice. Or maybe they just didn't care...

I followed along and set my towel up a little distance from theirs. I didn't want to be associated too closely with them.

"Are you going to be alright?" Andrew asked as he stood over my outstretched body and dropped a bottle of cold water onto my towel. He crossed his arms. He was expecting an answer.

I slid my sunglasses on and rolled over onto my stomach. "I'll be fine. Now get the fuck out of my sun."

"Fuck you."

I closed my eyes. We'd had our differences over the years, but Andrew had been there for me after I lost Amy. The guy might have a heart after all.

I raised my head, resting my chin on my hands, and smiled over at him. He smiled back at me and flipped me the *fuck you* finger. Ah, yes, brotherly love ...priceless.

As it turned out, the sun was what I needed. My tan had taken a serious hit, because of my self-imposed quarantine, and this felt damn good, the smell of tanning lotion and fries transporting me back to simpler times. Growing up in a beach resort meant a lot of time spent on the sand, first with my family, then friends...

I sighed. Then with Amy.

Fucking get over it.

"Hey, your back is burning," a guy's voice stated softly above me.

"I must've fallen asleep," I said as I rolled over onto my back and propped myself up on my elbows. I blinked to clear my vision. My initial view consisted of a pair of extremely tanned bare feet, adorned in those braided friendship bracelets you saw swarms of people wearing.

Then I looked up.

Holy fuck ...and yummy.

The guy staring down at me ...my age, and seriously hot, in a gorgeous and sultry kind of way. He looked familiar.

"Do I know you from somewhere?" I asked as I willed my cock to behave itself. Lying stretched out on my back in a pair of flimsy swim shorts was not the best cover.

"Name's Jake."

Jake brushed his hand up through his hair and my heart almost stopped. The action had revealed the thick, dark patch of hair under his arm, and caused his pecs to flex deliciously.

"I disc jockey over at *Crush*," Jake continued. "I saw you there the other night." His face lit up with a smile that restarted my sputtering heart and predictably warmed my balls. "You were pretty enthralled with what I was doing."

I allowed a small gasp of a laugh to escape. Yeah, that's definitely where I'd seen him before.

The night Amy dumped me, before she'd dumped me, we'd gone to *Crush* to do some drinking and dancing. I'd spent most of the night ogling the DJ instead, something Amy brought up, repeatedly, whilst screaming at me in the parking lot afterward.

Before she'd taken off in her car, Amy had told me she knew, that she'd probably always known, and I that needed to stop lying to myself.

I knew my attraction to guys ran way deep. Far deeper than I'd ever cared to admit, but how do you stop doing something you've done all your life?

Pretending to be straight had eclipsed every other aspect of my life for as long as I could remember.

So how do I stop?

I studied Jake's face watching me…

Fuck, he was hot, and I was single again.

I smiled.

Jake is how you stop lying to yourself.

"I do a bit of mixing myself." I blushed, embarrassed I'd even mentioned it, but I needed to say something. "Nothing like what you do at the club, of course."

"So, that's what you were staring at the other night at the club?" Jake grinned. "My mixing board?" He wasn't buying it, and I was glad he wasn't.

I let my gaze wander freely over his body, enjoying the way his little, fuchsia shorts clung to his sleek thighs, and cupped tight to his cock and balls, the ridge of his cockhead clearly visible...

"Yeah ...no," I said and laughed, unable to peel my gaze away from Jake's hand as he swept it across his smooth muscular chest, then thumbed one of his nipples.

I licked my lips.

"Do you want to get out of here?" Jake asked. "I live in that house right there." He pointed to an estate bordering the beach. "We could get out of the sun."

I nodded silently, sprung to my feet, and grabbed my towel to shield the rest of the beach from being subjected to my growing erection. I'd never *been* with a guy before, aside from a few drunken make-out sessions, but my nervousness didn't appear to be having a detrimental effect on what Jake's hard gorgeous body was doing to mine.

My cock pulsed against my body, seeking to escape from the mesh prison of my swim shorts.

Fucking hell ...what am I going to tell my brother?

"Andrew," I said, tossing a heap of sand at my brother's chest with my foot. "I'm going to take off for a while."

"Sure," Andrew said and opened his eyes. His gaze drifted between Jake and me. "Where are you going?"

"Jake here is a DJ ...he's going to show me his equipment."

A blinding flush rose in my face.

I hadn't meant to say it quite like that, but the slip amused my brother immensely.

"His equipment, hey?" Andrew said, smirking.

"Fuck off, Andrew," I replied. I wanted to cross my arms in annoyance, but my hard-on wasn't in the mood to wane, so I kept my towel clenched in front of my body instead.

Andrew's expression changed and became serious. "Sorry, but you walked right into that." He looked at Jake and sighed, then returned his attention to me. "Alright, so I'll see you later." He reached for my leg and brushed his hand along it, lingering at my ankle.

"Play safe, alright?" he whispered, staring up at me.

"Yeah, sure …," I replied, mildly confused. My brother had never given me any indication he knew I liked guys.

Gary snorted in amusement and tucked his hand behind his head. Under his breath, he muttered the word *finally*, sending Matt into a fit of quiet giggles.

Fuck, does everyone know?

"You can throw your towel down over there," Jake said, pointing to one of the stools lining the massive island in the middle of his kitchen. "Can I get you a drink?"

"A beer would be great."

I draped my towel over a stool. Jake already knew I was turned on. It was pointless hiding it. The sight of his DJ equipment set up in the living room distracted me though.

"Do you live here alone?" I asked as I slid into a chair facing a bank of computer screens and various pieces of midi equipment.

Jake wandered up beside me, set my beer down, and brushed his hand back and forth across my bare shoulders. My gut tightened as he massaged the muscles at the base of my neck.

"Sort of," Jake replied finally, removing his hand from my neck. "It's my parents' house, but they're away for six months, so I moved in." The sound of him laughing reverberated through me as he leaned against my shoulder. "Saves on rent and I'm closer to the beach."

"So I can cruise for hot guys at will," he added, his voice sounding sullied."

"Is that a regular thing for you?" I turned enough to look at him.

Jake straightened up and brushed his hand across his mouth.

"What? Cruising for guys?" he replied. "Not really. I was on my way to the corner store and thought I recognized you."

"On your way to the corner store." I crossed my arms, pretending to be put off. "By way of the beach."

"Yeah, I needed …milk. Or something."

"Mm …hm." I turned back to face the screens. "So, can you show me a few things on here?"

"Sure." Jake edged in closer, turned the computer on, and began setting up a file for me to play with. The skin of his shoulder as he typed, brushed my cheek, and I breathed in the scent of his sun-warmed body. I wanted to lick him all over, starting at the crease of his underarm where the aroma would be deepest.

I inhaled heavily. "Jake?"

"Mm …hm?"

"You smell really good," I said, dismissing the software displaying on the screen.

Jake grinned at me with a seductively devious glint. "I thought you were interested in my music software."

"Right now, I'm more interested in your hardware."

I know …corny, but it seemed appropriate given the fact Jake's nut-sack was pressed against my elbow and his stiffening cock was riding my forearm.

"I was hoping you'd say that," Jake replied, while grinding harder against my arm, his little fuchsia shorts bunching and rolling against my skin, catching the tiny hairs. He surprised me when he grasped my elbow firmly and hauled me out of my seat.

"Let's head over to the sofa," Jake said as he steered me toward it. We fell onto the cushions with me on top of him. I immediately attacked his mouth. Jake's lips were hot and moist, and hungry. There was no possible way I could get enough of him.

So fucking hot.

I'd longed to be with a guy like Jake, a guy that could show me what I'd been missing out on. I dove deeper into his mouth, our tongues sparring for dominance, tasting everything, consuming each other. I groaned in unison with him as our bodies crushed together. It was the most intense kiss I'd ever experienced, and the heat being generated by it was near suffocating.

Jake's hands were all over my back, exciting my skin, pulling me closer …kneading my flesh. I surged forward, held Jake against the cushions, and ground my rock-hard dick against his stomach. He thrust up against me, ran his hands down my back into my swim shorts, then slipped past the waistband and grabbed my ass.

I arched my back and tipped my ass up further, anxious for his touch. Jake slid a finger down my crease and teased the edge of my hole, massaging it gently. The sensation sent jolts of desperate need shuddering through my body. I ran my hands through his hair, then grasped his face, and clung to him. I ground against him harder as I kissed his neck and throat …wanting more.

Please give me more.

Jake gripped my shoulders and held me at bay.

"Let's see this ass of yours," he said, pushing me to my feet.

My fingers struggled with the ties of my swim shorts, frantic to comply. My only desire at that moment was to please him …to give Jake what he wanted. To let him do whatever he wanted with my body.

Finally undoing the ties, I hauled my shorts off, let them fall to the floor, and stepped out of them. My breath caught, sharp, almost in fear as Jake shoved me roughly toward the sofa. I'd fantasized about this, having a guy handle me hard.

I climbed onto the dark, brown leather sofa and kneeled on the cushions, my cock drooling slick pre-cum onto the fabric. I tilted my ass up to display my hole.

"Fuck, that's a hot ass," Jake said as he ran his palms up my thighs and onto my smooth muscular glutes. He kneaded them roughly and landed a light smack on one. I gasped in surprise but hoped he'd do it again.

I peered over my shoulder as Jake circled around behind me. Watching Jake was like witnessing a hunter eyeing his prey. It made me nervous but excited. My throbbing cock released a new thread of pre-cum, dripping and pooling onto the cushion beneath me.

"You like it?" I asked after catching his gaze.

"I fucking love it." Jake licked his thumb and traced it around the rim of my hole, then pressed against it hard enough to make the ache in my balls almost unbearable. I gripped tight to the sofa as Jake pried my crease open and thrust his tongue into my warm, anxious hole.

I gasped, almost to the point of passing out as the tip of Jake's wet tongue probed deeper, then flicked lightly, his hot breath drifting heavy down the dampening flesh of my thighs.

"You like that?" Jake asked between assaults.

"Fuck …yeah!" I reached back and grasped Jake's hair, hauling him closer. My reward was Jake shoving his tongue so far into my ass that I thought for sure he'd lose it.

Jake backed off and alternated between thrusting, then tasting and grunting happily as he probed and licked at my hole. I was about to reach for my dick when Jake pulled it through my legs from behind. The sensation of him sucking my cockhead almost did me in.

I bit into the cushions of the sofa, trying to temper my reaction.

"Mm …you taste amazing," Jake said, then went back to sucking and playing with my cock. He released it to attack my ass, his tongue licking wide swaths across my rim, teasing it.

My cock jumped and tapped my stomach as Jake spat into my hole and massaged his pointer finger inside, rotating it until I groaned.

"Fuck, yeah." I squirmed, arching my back to tempt him further. I needed him to fuck me. I looked back over my shoulder, caught Jake's gaze, and licked my lips.

Jake grinned. "Not yet, baby."

I lowered my head onto my arms. My body was positively vibrating with need. I wasn't in the mood to wait any longer. I needed to feel Jake's dick filling my ass.

I peered back at Jake in time to see him remove his swim shorts.

Fuck…

"That's a big dick," I said dumbly, then blushed.

"Mm …," Jake replied, slapping his meat against his hand. The sound drove every inhibition right out of me. I turned, still kneeling on the sofa, and wrapped my hand around Jake's tight, hot cock. I mouthed the head first, licking the slit and tasting the clear fluid of arousal, then circled my tongue all the way around the ridge. This was my first cock and I wanted to enjoy it. Jake's hand brushed through my hair. "You look so sexy down there."

I gazed up at him as I slid his cock past my lips. His hips hitched upward and he grabbed a fistful of my hair. I sucked hard as I pulled his cock back out of my mouth, and used my hand to pump it. He tasted fantastic. I licked at the head, then took him back in.

"That's right," Jake said. "Suck that big cock." He grasped tight to my head and forced his dick further into my throat. I coughed and choked, sputtering, but it felt fucking good.

I grabbed onto Jake's hips in order to keep from falling off the edge of the sofa each time he rocked away from me. His hand caressed my spine from shoulders to ass as he jammed his cock deeper, grunting and swearing, then his hand came down hard on my ass.

Yes, finally...

"You like that bitch?" Jake asked as he stretched forward to stroke my ass cheek. His fingers brushed tenderly across my skin. A tingle of pure warmth flooded my cock as Jake's hand came down again, stinging my sweat dampened skin.

I moaned around his dick as I continued to bob on it, slurping and sucking, then I backed off and lapped at Jake's cockhead while I jacked him.

Jake's hand snaking and tightening around my throat startled me at first, but as he hauled me up, I relaxed. Jake liked it rough and I didn't have an issue with that. I'd known the guy less than a half-hour, but I had a sense I could trust him.

Jake maneuvered me onto the arm of the sofa, lengthwise, stretching me out on my back. I reached over my head to brace myself against the wall in anticipation of Jake finally ramming his cock into me, but he wasn't finished playing with me yet.

My eyes rolled back in my head, in desperation as Jake hauled me closer to the front edge of the sofa's armrest. He hitched my legs up, and thrust his tongue into my ass, then sucked each of my balls into his mouth, in turn, rolling them over with his tongue, wetting them.

Jake's wet finger pressed deep into my ass, thrusting and retreating, gracing the gland within. It was infuriatingly close to what I wanted.

"Jake …" I reached for his arm to haul him closer, so I could grab his hip. "Please. I want you to fuck me."

"You're an anxious little bitch, aren't you?" Jake stepped closer, teasing me with his cock by smacking it against my thighs. He brushed it around my hole, applying enough pressure to make my stomach clench with expectation, then nothing.

Jake leaned over me, rubbing my hole with his finger and kissed me. He tasted so fucking good, the lingering taste and aroma of my own body heavy on his tongue.

Fuck me. Please fuck me.

My ass clenched, painfully, wanting to be filled, needing to be filled by Jake's huge fucking cock. I reached for it, wrapped my fingers around its girth, and stroked it, wanting to make it mine. I'd never wanted anything more than I wanted his cock in my ass, to feel it caressing my insides.

I shivered as Jake released me.

Jake's mouth closing around my dick caught me off guard. It was official …Jake was attempting to drive me insane. I scrubbed my hands across my face and clenched my teeth as I rode the undulating wave of aching need building in my gut.

Fuck, I can't stand it any longer.

"Jake, please," I pleaded. "I need you to fuck me."

Jake laughed and nodded, then reached for a ticker-tape length of condom packages. It appeared he was expecting a busy summer between gigs at the club.

I grinned, then licked my lips. I wasn't sure what to expect. I regularly played with an assortment of dildos, slicking them with lube and pumping them into my ass as I jerked off.

This wasn't anything like that. The sensation of a real cock being guided by warm hands into my ass, then sliding into place…

"Fuck!" I reached back for the wall and bit my bottom lip, enjoying the exhilaration of the burn. I nodded to Jake to start fucking me, but then I reached for his hips, stopping him.

"Are you alright?" Jake asked, genuine concern clouding his eyes.

"Yeah." I squirmed closer to him and lifted my feet onto Jake's shoulders. I needed him to go deep. I wanted to feel him in my throat. His cool balls came to rest on my crease, then retreated.

The first thrust almost made me scream at him to stop. I looked at the ceiling as the next thrust came, then closed my eyes. There were tears collecting in them.

I released the breath I'd been holding and relaxed. A few more thrusts and a wave of pleasure overcame me. Jake's cock felt amazing each time it plunged into me then withdrew.

Fuck.

Why did I wait so long to do this?

Jake gripped onto my thighs, adjusted his stance, and increased his pace and ferocity. The sofa shook, slamming against the wall.

I licked my lips and groaned.

Fuck. Me.

"You like that?" Jake asked as he fucked me harder.

"Fuck, yeah." I shifted my ass to raise it up a bit. Jake's cock went deeper, painful at first, then nothing but pure ecstasy. I could stay like this forever, fucking. I braced myself against the wall, so Jake's forceful assault wouldn't shift me away from him.

Jake groaned as he slammed me harder and faster.

My mind reeled. "Harder …fuck. Don't stop." My entire body quaked, my ass jiggling with the force. "Harder… God." I reached for Jake's face as he leaned into me, wanting our bodies to merge as his mouth enveloped mine. The kiss was urgent and furious—desperate. He grabbed my face and spat into my mouth, then attacked it again.

Damn, that's hot.

"Here," Jake stopped and lifted me straight off the arm of the sofa, and dropped his ass onto a cushion with me in his lap facing him, still impaled on his cock. I reached behind him and gripped the frame of the sofa, attempting to gain leverage as I pumped up and down.

It made a change from being pounded. Still felt great, but I was able to catch my breath. I rolled my head back, enjoying the rhythm of our bodies colliding.

Jake's hands slipped under my ass to help support me.

"You like riding my cock?" he asked.

I leaned in and kissed him. His upper lip was sweaty and slick. I licked the salty taste from it. "Yeah. I love it."

"Turn around. Facing away from me."

I cringed as I stood and Jake's cock pulled out of my ass. I needed it back where it belonged, but I had to wait as Jake changed out the condom.

As soon as he was done, I slipped back onto his shaft, sighing with satisfaction, then leaned back against Jake's chest. I felt his heart beating rapidly behind me. I reached back for him and ran my fingers into his hair as seductive gusts of his hot breath dampened my cheek.

The rolling movement of Jake's thrusting hips jammed his dick deep into my gut. I held steady in order to enjoy each penetrating jolt. I was getting close, and by the sound of Jake's rapid breathing, he was too.

"I want to cum," I whispered in Jake's ear.

Jake groaned. "You're so fucking sexy." He kissed my cheek and slowed his pace. "On your back."

I climbed off and stretched out on the sofa, parting my legs and reaching for him. This was all coming to an end far too soon, but I really needed to cum, and I wanted Jake to force it from my body with his cock. I'd dreamed of cumming with a hard dick up my ass, pounding me into submission, more times than I'd ever had sex with Amy.

I encased my cock, stroking lightly as Jake slid back into me. He was slower this time, delivering a steady, deliberate massage, driving me crazy in all new ways.

I groaned and fought for breath as Jake rocked my body.

"You seem to be liking that," Jake whispered.

"It feels really good." I gasped as my gut twinged. "I'm close." I closed my eyes, concentrating on the overall sensation. It started low in my balls, tightening them, then I felt my dick harden and pulse in my hand.

The first shot hit my face and I panted through it, licking my lips. "Fuck …" I opened my mouth for the next one, catching a bit on my tongue. I gripped onto Jake's arm as the rest of my load hit my chest, then my stomach. I milked the last drop, then released my cock, and licked the streams of cum from my hand, making sure not to miss any.

"Fuck, that's hot," Jake said as he pulled his cock out of me, yanked the condom off, and flung it onto the floor. He rose onto his knees and hovered over my stomach as he jacked steadily on his cock, his fist twisting and pulling on the head with each stroke.

The sound erupting from his chest as he brought himself closer, cranked me right back up again. My dick twitched and hardened, anxious for more. There was a strong possibility I wouldn't be headed back to the beach anytime soon.

"Fuck, yeah." I brushed my hands up Jake's chest, pinching at his nipples. "I want to see you cum."

"Yeah?"

"Mm …hm." I bit my bottom lip, fascinated by the building tension. I wanted Jake to cum all over me.

"I'm cumming." Jake's head lolled back and his body convulsed steadily as he shot his warm load onto my chest.

"Fuck," I groaned as I watched the expression of ecstasy on Jake's face. I definitely wanted to see that a few more times. He grinned at me as I shifted beneath him, then his body relaxed and he hovered closer. He gently kissed me.

"Hey," Jake said as he pulled back. "I never caught your name."

I smiled and brushed my hand across his glistening, sweaty chest. "Connor."

"Well, Connor. I'd like to see you again."

I pulled Jake closer. "I'd like that."

Maybe going to the beach wasn't so bad after all.

Submission

The energy of the music is what drove most people to the doors of the club *Crush,* and that was on account of Jake and his crazy mixing skills. I still couldn't believe Jake had managed to swing me a job behind the bar, not on some shitty weekday shifts, but on weekends.

It made me wonder who Jake had fucked to secure me the spot.

Not that I cared, of course. We weren't together.

Jake and I had only fucked around that one afternoon. Several times, mind you, but that had happened last week and I hadn't talked to him since. Not until he'd phoned me about the job.

I looked toward the DJ booth as I emptied the dishwasher, and caught Jake's attention. I winked at him playfully, which made him grin.

There was a strong possibility my job security was going to rely heavily on my job performance, and not the kind happening by mixing drinks behind the bar.

I hadn't told Jake that the afternoon he'd picked me up at the beach, and fucked me in every possible position I ever could've imagined, was my first time with a guy.

He hadn't suspected, and I wasn't about to tell him.

A tingle ran down my spine and furled in my gut, stiffening my cock as I remembered my first time. Jake was an incredible lover. If I had to let him fuck me every night after work to keep this job, I would have absolutely no objections.

My new boss, Dylan, clapped his hands in front of my face. "Hey, Connor. Snap out of it."

"Sorry." I got back to work drying and setting out the rest of the beer glasses I'd unloaded. I was about to pop them into the fridge to cool them off when Dylan nudged me.

"Can you head downstairs and check on that finicky keg I told you about?" he asked as he pulled one of the tap levers multiple times to no avail. "The fucking thing isn't working again."

"Yeah, sure."

I wasn't a fan of scurrying around in basements. Especially dark, creepy basements beneath noisy nightclubs where no one would hear you scream if you were attacked by some random drunk wandering patron. Or worse. Some kind of ghostly apparition.

The club *was* in a centuries old industrial building.

I stuffed my hands into my jean's pockets as I navigated my way through the basement to the back where the kegs were hooked up, not wanting my digits trailing at my sides in the near darkness. An icy cold gush of air drifted around my body, tickling my ears and disturbing the delicate threads of a nearby cobweb.

I shivered. Goosebumps puckered the skin on my forearms and frightened the little hairs on the back of my neck to full attention as my mind leapt to all sorts of crazy conclusions regarding the cause of the disturbance in the otherwise dank motionless air occupying the basement.

Stop it.

I really needed to think about curtailing my appetite for late night *ghost hunting* shows.

I jumped as a loud sound from overhead reverberated through the floor above me. Judging by how far I'd walked,

I placed myself somewhere beneath the DJ booth. Jake must've hopped down from his post to get a drink or hit the washroom for a piss.

I swore as my foot connected with one of the heavy beer kegs. The image of Jake snaking his gorgeous cock out of his pants in the washroom above had totally distracted me. I'd spent hours worshipping that cock. If I concentrated, I could still feel its smooth hardness sliding through my lips and caressing my tongue.

Fuck.

Cut it out.

I needed to concentrate on fixing the keg. I sat on the edge of the first keg and leaned sideways to reach the temperamental one. I could work on one of these things in my sleep, so my mind wandered as I shut the valve and pulled the attachment apart.

I'd known for a long time I was gay. Even back in high school, I'd made a point of joining every possible sports team and taking physical education long past the grade required for graduation. All for the purpose of being able to sneak glimpses of other guys' cocks in the shower, so I could collect plenty of visuals to jerk off to later.

But that was before I'd discovered the plethora of gay porn available on the internet. Unearthing this treasure trove had taken me to the very edge of ecstasy for two reasons. One …I no longer had to play asinine sports, which I'd hated with a passion for as long as I could remember, and two …I could watch two, or more, guys fucking each other as I jerked off.

Priceless. Absolutely fucking priceless. I could kiss the guy that invented the internet.

A measure of beer spilled down my wrist.

Stupid fucking thing.

I tapped the plastic hosing on the edge of the keg, then peered into it. It was completely clear. The problem had to be with the valve. It most likely needed to be replaced, but club owners were notoriously cheap when it came to maintaining equipment. I could probably do a temporary fix on it myself. I'd passed a toolbox on the way in. If I pulled the valve apart, cleaned all the crud out of it, then put it back together, it should work for a while longer.

I stood and turned straight into Jake.

"Holy fuck, Jake!"

Jake smiled. Immediately disarming me and sending a warm tingle through to my balls.

Fuck he's hot.

"Sorry," Jake said. "I thought you would've heard me."

"I was a little distracted."

"By these kegs?" Jake knocked on one, filling the basement with a baritone wave of sound.

I blushed.

Luckily, the lighting in the basement was dim, or I would've been blushing deeper in embarrassment for …blushing.

Shit.

Jake's close proximity to my body turned my insides all wobbly, but I needed to get back to work. "I need to fix this valve," I said, skirting around Jake to go find the toolbox.

"Why?"

"Because it's broken." I threw the toolbox down on the ground next to the keg. Jake stopped me from lifting the valve.

"What will happen if you don't fix it," he asked.

"We would have no amber ale on tap."

"So …"

I shrugged.

"Dylan would be pissed," I added.

"No, I wouldn't," Dylan said as he stepped up behind me.

My heart hammered up into my throat and I grabbed onto the nearest support post to steady myself. My nerves were officially shot.

"Fuck, you guys," I said. "Could you cough or something instead of sneaking up on me and scaring me half to death?"

"I don't know," Jake replied, moving closer and cupping my face in his hand. "I kind of like it when you're all flustered and scared like this." He brushed a thumb across my lips, then popped it into my mouth, hauling my jaw open and playing with my tongue. "What do you think, Dylan?"

"Mm ... let's see," Dylan said as the hardness of his jean covered cock pressed against the crease in my ass.

Oh fuck, yes.

I leaned my head back against Dylan's chest.

He was a good foot and a half taller than me, and I fit perfectly into the curve beneath his chin. Derek swept his hands up under my shirt, one running a line up the center of my chest to my throat, while the other encircled my waist, holding me in place against his body.

I moaned softly in anticipation.

Dylan's hot breath puffed across the top of my hair as he laughed. "You were right, Jake. "Your friend appears to be a bit of a slut." He rocked his shaft harder against me and I groaned, then reached behind me to grab Derek's ass and haul him closer.

"Greedy too," Dylan added.

"He is a bit," Jake said, then smiled as he rubbed his

hands up my chest, tweaking at my nipples through the thin material of my shirt.

I pressed my ass back against Dylan's body and ground against him. Jake's touch had ramped up my desire. I wanted to feel the full length of Dylan's hardening cock jammed against my ass.

Dylan moaned a soft breath into my ear and my cock stiffened, wetting the inside of my boxers as I pictured what these two gorgeous men were going to do to me.

I'd never thought of myself as a submissive person until I'd started fantasizing about having a guy fuck me for real. Watching scene after scene unfold on my computer screen every night had fueled a craving in me that couldn't be satisfied by my hand and a chunk of rubbery, fake dick.

The very idea of turning my body over and allowing a guy to take and give pleasure, from and to me, had begun to occupy my every thought when it came to sex.

It was around that same time when my relationship with my girlfriend, Amy, went south. Pretending to be straight had run its course. It wasn't working for me anymore.

The cold air of the basement whispered past my taut nipples as I raised my arms over my head and allowed Jake to remove my shirt. I leaned back heavier against Dylan's chest as Jake made short work of discarding my jeans, boxers, and my shoes and socks.

The cold, rough cement of the floor sent chills up my spine through my bare feet. I groaned as my teeth chattered. Nervous, but excited. I was standing in the basement of a busy nightclub, where any number of people might walk in and see me, naked and cold, waiting to be used.

Jake motioned for me to place my hands on my head.

"He's pretty," Dylan said as he circled around me,

running his hands all over my chest and down my back onto my ass. He gave it one sharp strike with his hand. I groaned, then shifted my position slightly to regain my balance as Dylan's calloused hand encased my semi-erect cock and jacked it a few times, handling it much rougher than I was used to.

I closed my eyes and steadied my breathing.

Just breathe.

My heart jumped when I heard the clang of a keg being unhooked behind me. I peered over my shoulder, but Dylan swiveled my face back to look at him.

"Don't be doing that," Dylan said as he gripped my chin in one hand. "All the nice people want to see your face."

What?

I cut my gaze through the darkness behind Dylan. There were at least ten people standing in the shadows. This had been planned. The malfunctioning keg. The presence of Jake and Dylan in the basement. My gut tightened as my cock twitched, which sent a tremor up my spine.

Holy fuck.

My breathing sped up and I dug my fingers into the mass of unruly curls on my head.

"You up for a bit of fun?" Dylan asked me.

I licked my lips and nodded my head as I scanned the observers for anyone I knew. I lowered my gaze to stare at the floor. Even if there was someone, it was too late to turn back.

My body was aching to be used.

"Fuck!" I cringed in shock as an unexpected sensation ran down my back. I almost stepped forward, away from what was happening, but then corrected my response and stood still as Jake poured a second stream of beer across my shoulders from the container we used to bleed the lines.

Little rivulets traced my collarbone and ran down the center of my chest, but the bulk of the pungent ale found its way down my back to the crease in my ass. It ran through between my legs and dripped off my balls and the tip of my cock.

The chill air of the basement kissed my wet skin, making my muscles clench and jump as they tried to maintain my body temperature. "Bend over," Jake said. "Grab your ankles."

I did what I was told, but I shook with apprehension. I trusted Jake implicitly, but I knew absolutely nothing about Dylan. The sound of Dylan laughing made me jump. He was no longer in front of me. Another measure of beer poured over my ass. This time it traveled along my spine, soaking my hair, and curled its way around my face to drip off the tip of my nose.

Dylan laughed. "You really are a dirty little slut, aren't you?"

I nodded my head as I licked the beer from my upper lip, then closed my eyes as I tried to decipher the whispered murmur of a heated discussion happening behind me. My back and hamstrings were beginning to ache, and I desperately wanted to either stand up or kneel, but I held my position, adjusting the grip on my ankles. My eyes popped open when Jake spoke.

"Absolutely not," he said to Dylan, then tapped me on the ass. "Stand up."

Oh god. What did he just save me from?

I straightened up and cringed as my back muscles protested the change in position. I reached for Jake to support me and shivered. Jake pulled me in against him, offering some warmth.

"You alright?" he whispered in my ear.

I nodded and ran my hands through his hair, closing the minuscule gap between our bodies.

"If you want us to stop, tell me," Jake added. "I'll call Dylan off and get you out of here."

I shook my head. "I want this. You know I do."

Jake cupped my face. "You are so fucking sexy," he whispered against my lips.

"Get over here," Dylan said as he spun me around. He unzipped the front of his pants, retrieved his cock, and pushed me to my knees. I stroked the shaft of his thick cock with my hand first, judging its size, before tasting the flared, angry head with the flat of my tongue.

The taste of the velvety surface was different from Jake's, more pungent, but fucking amazing in its own way. I sucked the entire head into my mouth, humming around it in enjoyment.

"You like that, bitch?" Dylan growled from beneath an expression hooded with desire.

I tapped his rock hard length against my tongue, slapping it in the pool of moisture I'd collected as I peered up into his face. I nodded my head, took his cock into my mouth, and pressed it against the back of my throat, then sucked it all the way back along its length, ending at the slit.

Dylan groaned and rocked away, then took a few steps back and sat on one of the kegs. I crawled forward on all fours, cursing the uneven surface of the cement floor as it dug into my flesh. I slid my mouth back over Dylan's cock while keeping my hands on the floor.

The cool air tickled my balls as I savored every inch of Dylan's dick, from the coarse, curly hairs at the root to the drooling slit at the tip. I tipped my ass up and separated my legs. The thought of being so exposed, so submissive as people watched, sent a fresh surge to my cock, tightening it.

My hole puckered and released with excitement.

I trembled as a wave of need overtook me.

Oh. God. Please.

I moaned around Dylan's shaft as I swayed my hips back and forth, my body aching to be touched. I reached through my legs, cradled my balls, and brushed my index finger along my taint.

When Dylan didn't stop me, I slipped my finger into my mouth, wet it, then pressed the tip into my ass. I tucked my hips up and struggled to keep my balance as I buried the entire length of my finger deep inside.

I groaned, vibrating through the sensation, and dropped Dylan's cock from my mouth.

"Fucking greedy little …!" Dylan grabbed a handful of my hair and stuffed his cock back in my mouth, burying my face in his pubes as he jammed his cockhead down my throat.

I choked and pulled off, then regained my balance by grabbing onto his thighs with both hands. I spat a long vicious line of saliva onto his cock.

Fuck …sorry.

I used the slick mess to jack Dylan a few times, while I checked over my shoulder to see what Jake was doing. His jeans were undone and his shirt pulled up and over his head to expose his chest. He stroked his cock with strong steady movements that were flexing his bicep with a seductive precision only Jake could pull off.

"Help me out," Dylan said to Jake. "Maybe you can teach this little slut some manners."

Jake grinned at me. "Doubt it."

Smiling, I stroked my hands up Jake's thighs, then kissed the material covering them. I peeled Jake's jeans open further and shimmied them off his hips. His clean musky taste permeated my senses as I extended my tongue to tickle the dark, sweat slickened hairs surrounding Jake's cock.

I sucked one of his balls into my mouth as I reached around and traced my fingers up and down the center seam that ran along the crease of Jake's ass. I'd lost count of the number of times I'd dreamt of gaining access to that crease, but Jake had told me he didn't bottom for anyone, ever.

Still caressing his ass, I ran my tongue around Jake's cockhead, then capped my mouth over it, while swirling my tongue along the ridge. I sucked on the thick head, then released it, and used my tongue to wet Jake's shaft on one side.

I sucked the head of Jake's cock past my wet lips, bobbed quick and hard on it, then slicked up the length of his cock, while I kept a tight grip on it.

Jake placed his hand on my shoulder, his eyes closed, his breathing heavy. I grabbed on to his ass to pull him closer as I buried my face against his body, his cock filling my throat. I held myself there for a moment, his coarse manicured hairs tickled my nose. I coughed and gasped for breath, then sucked his dick all the way back out to the tip.

I wiped the back of my hand across my face and looked up at him.

"Fuck, that's good," Jake said as he brushed his fingers through my hair, then grabbed handfuls of it and rocked his hips, sending his cock pulsing and hardening between my lips, caressing the roof of my mouth. I encased his shaft with my hand, gliding the smooth skin back and forth over the hard member beneath its surface as I sucked at the head.

I ran my tongue along the slit, then pulled Jake's foreskin right up over the tip and sipped it closed with my lips. I tickled the puckered flesh with my tongue, then slid the excess skin back against Jake's body and jammed the full length of his cock into my throat.

Jake grabbed my shoulder and pulled me off.

"You're going to make me cum if you keep that up," he said, then patted my face, grinning down at me.

Dylan's hand raked through my hair and hauled me toward him. The sting of my hair being wrenched brought a few tears to my eyes, but I blinked them away and dove back on Dylan's cock.

"Good little slut," Dylan said but refused to relinquish his hold on my hair, preferring to sweep his other hand into it as well, which set me off balance.

I tried to arrange myself so the rough cement wasn't digging into my knees, but it was impossible to avoid the exposed aggregate at Dylan's feet.

"Hands and knees," Jake said from somewhere behind me.

I shivered. Not because I was bloody cold, which I was but because Jake had wandered out of my sightline. I placed my hands on the ground, and balanced myself on all fours, then filled my mouth with Dylan's dick as I listened for anything happening behind me.

I groaned and shifted. Not sure what I should be anticipating, the uncertainty encouraging my cock. It was poker hard and leaving a patterned trail of pre-cum on the dusty cold floor.

I shot forward and moaned around Dylan's cock as Jake's hand struck my backside, hard.

It stung deliciously.

Fuck yeah.

"You like that, you little slut?" Dylan tipped my head up to look at him. I hummed and nodded my approval. I pinched my eyes closed as Jake's hand warmed the other cheek.

Mm ...again.

I arched my back as much as I could while still bobbing up and down on Dylan's cock, anticipating more strikes. The soft touch of Jake's hand brushing past my balls made me jump, then my mind raced screaming through images of what I wanted him to do.

More ...do more.

"Uhm ..." I held Dylan's cock steady in my mouth, tonguing the thick vein running along the underside as I tried to collect myself.

Jake pulled my cock and balls through my legs from behind. He squeezed and tugged on them until my eyes watered, then his hand landed on my ass. My cock twitched, then drooled a new pool of pre-cum onto the floor, anxious for more of Jake's attention. A quick succession of alternating strikes warmed my ass, then stopped.

I dropped Dylan's cock from my mouth and spat on his shaft until it glistened with wetness. I stroked his length, twisting on the upstroke and enveloping the plum colored head in the extra skin. I sucked at the end, collecting the musky pre-cum, then let it settle in the curve of my tongue as I savored it. Dylan grunted his approval.

I swallowed and looked over my shoulder as Jake rolled a condom into place.

Finally.

"Lift him up," Jake said to Dylan.

Jake stepped closer and directed Dylan to hoist me up, so I could wrap my legs around Dylan's waist and my arms around his neck.

Once on his hips, Dylan sneered at me and snaked his face toward me to encase my mouth.

Fuck you.

I twisted my neck, deeking away from him. I had no intention of allowing Dylan to kiss me.

"Fucking bitch," Dylan growled in my ear.

Damn.

So much for job security.

I had a funny feeling I was unemployed again. Which was probably a good thing because I'd recognized a couple of fellow employees standing in the shadows of the basement with the others.

Andrew was going to be thrilled.

I clung to Dylan's body and tucked my face into his neck as Jake plastered his chest against my back and guided his cock toward my hole. He circled it a few times, smearing the cold lube around, then positioned himself. I shifted my ass, improving my angle and he slipped right in, his entire shaft ripping past my outer ring, straight into my gut.

A small mewling cry escaped my lips.

Ow. Fuck. Ow.

I reached back to ease Jake away but in doing so felt myself sliding further onto his cock, so I clambered back up Dylan's body and hung on. Dylan grunted with amusement and shifted his hands, peeling my ass cheeks open further, increasing the burn.

"Here we go, you little slut," Dylan hissed in my ear and bounced me down hard onto Jake's cock.

I shrieked and squirmed, clenching my eyes shut.

Fuck. Fuck. Fuck.

Oh fuck.

Jake's hot breath found the back of my neck and he kissed it as he settled his hands along my ribcage, redistributing Dylan's control somewhat.

"Come on, baby," Jake whispered in my ear. "You can take it. You like it rough." He kissed my ear. "I know you do."

I nodded my head.

Jake grunted, then licked and bit at my shoulder as Dylan pumped me up and down. I sucked in a shaky, wet breath and bit my bottom lip, fighting to stay above the pain.

After a few agonizing moments passed, it felt so fucking good, I forgot about Dylan and the onlookers, focused solely on Jake and his thundering heartbeat echoing throughout my body.

The pleasure-filled sound of Jake's voice as he licked and sucked at my ear, and the feel of Jake's body possessing me completely as he stroked my insides, was taking me beyond elation.

"Mm …fuck me, baby," I said, then grinned at the husky quality of my voice. Jake chuckled in my ear and I nuzzled further into Dylan's neck, the heat from being pressed between their two bodies finally warming my core.

I groaned and worked my ass, drawing and releasing Jake's cock to make the most of every thrust, by forcing his thick shaft against my prostate, again and again, building me up.

I sunk into Dylan's rhythm and let my mind go blank but was shaken from my trance when the ride became rougher, sending sharp pains up my spine as Dylan began to tire.

Jake pulled out and Dylan set me back on my feet.

"On your knees," Dylan demanded. "Hands behind you."

I looked at Jake and he nodded, so I did what I was told. I sunk to my knees and clasped my hands behind my back as I peered out at the people watching me.

Most were quietly observing, but there were a few guys trying to inconspicuously stroke their aroused cocks. A tingle of warmth crept from my balls to my own cock as I focused on them, wondering if watching me was going to make them cum.

I licked my lips.

The sensation of more beer being poured over my head caught me by surprise, restarting my shivering as the cold crept back in. I clenched my teeth to keep them from chattering.

Dylan circled around from behind me and tapped my face with his cock, smearing pre-cum on my cheek.

Fucking bastard.

"Open," he demanded and pressed his semi-erect cock hard against my lips. I sucked him in, then slipped the skin away from the soft head with my hand, tongued the slit, and sipped at the pungent flavor. "Mm—" I shuffled closer to get a better angle.

"Fuck yeah, bitch," Dylan grunted. "You want that cock, don't you?" He shoved my head until I looked up. "Tell me you want it."

"I want it," I said softly, not sure what Dylan wanted from me.

"Say it like you mean it."

I stroked my hand up and down his shaft a few times. I *did* want it. I wanted it in my mouth …in my ass, stroking me. Rubbing against my own cock …filling my hand.

I looked up as my chest heaved.

"I want it," I spoke clearly this time. "I want your cock."

Dylan sneered down at me and I encased his entire cock with my mouth and got to work, only relenting when Jake stroked his hand through my hair and turned my head to face him.

Jake was about to cum.

I tilted my head and extended my tongue as Jake struggled through the final moments before releasing his load. I managed to catch most of it on my tongue, but a significant amount ended up dripping from my face and the beer-soaked tendrils of my hair. I pushed some out of my mouth to coat my lips and chin, then swallowed the rest.

I sat back on my haunches and stared up at Dylan.

He smirked at me.

"My turn," he said as he motioned toward where the rest of the kegs were stored, then I was lifted off my feet. Jake at my shoulders and Dylan at my ankles. I hadn't realized how strong Jake was. Although, I should've suspected after the way he'd tossed me around at his house last week.

Fuck.

The cold hard ridges of the beer kegs dug into my tailbone and shoulder blades as they arranged me on top. My head hung over the edge of the last one in the line. Jake had rolled up his shirt to put under my head, so it wasn't as uncomfortable as it would have been without.

I reached back and steadied myself, clinging to Jake's pant legs as he fed me his cock. It was soft and warm. I circled my tongue around it, and nipped into the folds of his foreskin, then savored his unique taste. The toes of Dylan's heavy boots banged against the keg beneath my ass, disturbing the moment.

"Let's see this ass of yours," Dylan said, smacking at my thigh.

I lifted my legs from where they were hanging off the edge of the keg and tried to position myself, but the edge of the keg kept digging into my back, making it impossible.

Jake reached down my body, hooking my knees with his hands and hauled my legs up practically to my ears.

Oh god.

I closed my eyes.

Dylan drove into me, hard. I swallowed around Jake's cock, dispensing of the extra saliva. A small amount escaped and traveled across my cheek and into my hairline.

"Urhm …" I squeezed my eyes closed tight.

I exhaled and grunted as Dylan took over securing my legs and slammed into me.

My breath came back heated. Jake's balls were draped across the bridge of my nose, their weight kissing my cheeks, and for the most part, Jake's body was blocking out any light.

I inhaled the scent of him and relaxed.

Dylan's next thrust was pure warmth.

God, yeah. Harder.

I shifted my ass, accepting every penetrating jolt, and hummed around Jake's cock with contentment.

Mm …glorious.

Dylan picked up his pace, thrusting harder and faster, hammering my ass into submission.

Fuck, yes. That's it.

I reached up and pressed Jake away, letting his cock slip from my mouth.

"I want to cum," I said to him as I hauled on his arm to bring him closer. A flutter of nerves tickled my stomach as he leaned in, hovering over my mouth with his.

Jake grinned down at me. "Do you now?"

God, he's adorable.

I wrapped an arm around Jake's neck and pulled him down onto my mouth. It was pure heaven tasting him again. Feeling the texture of his tongue, the softness of his palette, and the strength of his lips, each of us taking and giving. Sharing everything.

Jake tore himself away, almost stumbling backward. He placed a firm hand on my chest as if to steady himself. His arm vibrated and shook with every angry thrust of Dylan's hips, but he didn't remove it. He just stared at me.

I blinked, confused, then ventured to engage my cock. I wrapped my hand around it, but Jake knocked my hand away. He wet his palm and caressed me with a caring but heated determination, his thumb and forefinger slipping smoothly along my shaft with the right amount of pressure.

I gripped Jake's wrist to stop him as my hips rocked up.

"Oh, fuck!" I released my load and grunted through every burst as Dylan's cock forced it from my body, coating Jake's thumb and fingers.

He continued stroking me until my cock became too sensitive to be touched.

I winked at him. "That was hot."

"Fuck, baby …," Jake said to me, then fell silent. He studied my face as he moved aside for Dylan to unload on me.

I extended my tongue, while I rubbed my hand up and down Dylan's thigh to encourage him but kept my eyes on Jake as he circled around to the other side of the kegs.

He looked fucking lost.

"Yeah, baby …I wanna see you cum," I said flatly to Dylan.

I flicked my attention to Dylan for a split second. He was focused purely on his cock, so I withdrew my tongue, closed my mouth, and went back to watching Jake.

"Fuck …I'm cumming," Dylan groaned, bucking, then shot thick ropes of cum onto the side of my face, wetting my eyelids and lips, as well as my cheek.

I wiped away what I could, and flicked it onto the floor. Jake looked away, slipped his shirt out from behind my head and pulled it back on, then started for the door.

"Jake?" I attempted to roll off the kegs, but my body objected, sending stabbing pains down my spine, up through my ass, and out to all my extremities.

Jake, please. No.

He wouldn't leave me here with Dylan, naked and freezing, covered in beer and cum with a bunch of strangers standing around gawking at me.

He wouldn't do that to me.

Would he?

I closed my eyes, covered my face with my arms, and let the shivering set in. It was one thing to be used. It was another thing entirely to be used and discarded.

The sound of Jake's voice in my ear startled me.

"I went to find some towels," Jake said as he stroked his fingers through my hair. "Let's dry you off and I'll take you home." He kissed my forehead. "Alright?"

He winked at me and stroked a thumb across my cheek. "Maybe run you through a hot shower?" He grinned. "I'll soap you up myself."

"I'd like that." I laid my hand on the one Jake was using to caress my face, nuzzled into it, and kissed his thumb.

"And then I think we need to talk, Connor."

Yeah...

I nodded.

We definitely needed to talk.

Confession

There was nothing in the fridge besides a loaf of white bread, a few condiments, and something that was completely unrecognizable, floating around in the bottom of the crisper drawer. Groceries were always a bit sparse right before my brother, Andrew was paid.

I felt bad. My inability to find a proper job and keep it for any length of time had really put my brother in a spot financially. I'd officially been living off his generosity for almost three months now, and he was getting sick of my mooching, a topic of many heated discussions.

I threw the fridge door closed, empty handed.

Now, what am I supposed to do?

I leaned over the back of the sofa, slid onto the seat cushions, and rolled onto my side. My shoulder blades and lower back were bruised and extremely tender, after being stretched out on those beer kegs last night, but they were the least of my worries.

As predicted, I was unemployed again.

I'd tried to explain to Andrew it wasn't entirely my fault I'd been fired from my position at *Crush* after only one night, but without being able to give him the full details of what had pissed my boss, Dylan, off so much, I came off sounding like an idiot. I had no plans of ever filling Andrew in on that little piece of information.

I'd blown Dylan, let him fuck me, and cum all over my face, but he'd been hung up on the fact I wouldn't let him kiss me. He'd had the nerve to call me a tease after what I'd let him and Jake do to me last night.

A tease? Fucking asshole.

I was comfortable being called a slut and a whore, it was a real turn on, but I was no tease. What kind of tease lets you strip them, soak them in beer, and use them to that extent?

Tease, huh.

Just because I wouldn't kiss him, the fucker had fired me. Talk about sexual harassment in the workplace.

I eased further into the cushions of the sofa and undid the Velcro fastener of my swim shorts. Andrew wasn't due home from work for a while yet, and the memory of everything that had happened to me last night was making me hard. I slipped my hand into my shorts and stroked my cock flat against my stomach.

I reached for the towel I'd left on the floor after my shower, spread it out on the cushions to protect them, then slipped my shorts completely off my ass, and lay down on my stomach.

Needing something to hold on to, I propped myself up on my elbows and pushed my fingers into the space between the last sofa cushion and the armrest. I thrust the hardening length of my cock between my body and the towel. The sensitive head slipped in and out of my foreskin. I set my forehead on the edge of the armrest, groaning, and bit my lip as my arousal increased.

This wasn't going to take long.

I shut my eyes and imagined it was Jake beneath me, that I was fucking him. I spit a wad of saliva onto a couple of my fingers and pressed them into my ass in one swift move. I loved the way it burned when I didn't ease my way in. I rocked my hips toward the towel with increasing force as I imagined Jake's voice calling my name, crying for me to fuck him harder.

I bent my free arm at the elbow and kissed at my sweat-dampened skin, envisaging it was Jake I was tasting, then slipped my tongue into the soft crook of my arm, dancing it into the heat.

Oh yeah ...fuck.

I tempered my cries against my arm, biting into my flesh as I jammed my hips forward and coated the towel and the flat of my stomach in a warm blanket of slippery release, each shudder reducing the friction, until the tip of my cock was too sensitive to continue.

Last night had worn me out sexually in some ways, like the need to have my ass full of cock, but in other ways, like the need to pump my cock into something substantial, I couldn't bypass the recurring desire, regardless of how many times I'd jacked off this morning.

God, Jake, where are you?

I buried my face in the cushion and slipped my fingers from my ass. I needed to talk to Jake, but I had no idea where he was. He'd been gone this morning by the time I woke up. I'd tried calling him but had only reached his voicemail with a message that his mailbox was full.

I pushed up onto my knees and used the towel to wipe down my stomach. The bathroom was definitely next on my agenda. I'd only just finished cleaning myself up when I heard Andrew's keys unlocking the front door. I scrambled back to the living room and shuffled some magazines around on the coffee table to make it look like I was tidying up.

My unemployment status automatically relegated me to the position of maid, but I was useless at it. I hadn't even managed to figure out how to do laundry. I always ended up sorting the clothes into far too many piles. Andrew had thrown a fit when he'd found out how much money I was pumping into the machines with the extra loads. If it hadn't been for the elderly lady down the hall taking pity on me, my brother and I would likely be walking around in dirty clothes.

As for the rest of the apartment, it was a mess, and not because I'm a slouch or ungrateful for everything my brother was doing for me. I was incredibly grateful, but I had a bad habit of becoming distracted. Usually by simple things. Like alphabetizing and categorizing my brother's vast vinyl record collection in new ways, or reorganizing the files on my computer to suit whatever my latest criteria quirk was. Nothing major. It was just time consuming.

"Hey, Andrew," I said as my brother wandered into the kitchen and slid a case of beer onto the counter. He didn't answer me. "How was work?"

"It was work, Connor. You should try it sometime."

Here we go again.

"Andrew, I'm really sorry about—"

Andrew slammed the fridge door closed and all the little magnets I'd arranged so meticulously fell to the floor. I moved to pick them up and fix them but then changed my mind. Andrew was eyeing me with a strange look on his face.

"Where were you *really* last night?" he asked. He leaned on the counter. I wasn't sure if he was angry or something else I couldn't quite place. Worried? Repulsed? Both?

Fuck.

"I told you. I was working at *Crush* last night," I answered.

"That guy Jake from the beach got you the job."

"Yeah."

"As a bartender."

"Yeah." I moved toward Andrew, but he skirted around me. He was freaking me out. "Why all the questions?"

"Because …" Andrew tucked his arms across his chest. He looked like he was about to throw up.

Oh my god. He knows. How does he know?

"What did you hear?" I asked, wanting to get it over with. Maybe he hadn't heard too many details. Although, what part of letting two guys fuck me in front of a group of onlookers could be sugar coated enough to sound like a normal activity.

"Was it you?" Andrew's gaze flicked up onto my face, then shot away. He couldn't even stand to look at me. "In the basement …with those guys. Was it you?"

Now, I probably could've said *no* at this point, but I was fairly certain Andrew already knew the answer to his question. Someone he knew had seen me.

I sunk onto one of the kitchen stools.

"Andrew—"

"Don't fuck around, Connor. Just tell me if it was you."

I ducked my eyes. "Yeah." I looked up, meeting his gaze. "Yeah, it was me." I slid off the stool. "Look, Andrew—"

"I don't want to hear it." Andrew dragged his hands through his hair, then gripped at his head as his face turned a horrendous crimson. He balled his hands into fists, then slammed them onto the counter. "What the fuck were you thinking? Do you actually get off on sick shit like that?"

My only response was a deep sigh because the answer was *absolutely*. I absolutely got off on sick shit like that. Jake must've sensed that about me during our marathon sex session last week when we'd first met. I'd let him do things to me that I'd only dreamed of. I hadn't even had to ask. Jake had instinctively known what I needed.

"Is that why you were fired?" Andrew asked.

"Not exactly."

God, not now.

Someone was ringing up from the lobby.

"It's Mom and Dad," Andrew said, pressing the key on the phone to let them into the building.

My stomach lurched. "You called them about this?"

"No, you moron." Andrew shoved me on his way to the front door. "The barbecue is tonight."

Shit. Totally forgot.

The annual barbecue had been an institution in my family since Andrew, my sister, Karen, and I were kids. Now that we'd all moved out, the barbecue rotated from one family member to the next. It had been my mom's idea, which would have worked out fine, except none of us kids ever had enough money, so my parents still ended up footing the entire food bill.

"What do you mean by *not exactly*?" Andrew asked as he studied me from his place beside the front door where he was waiting for my parents to emerge from the elevator.

"I wouldn't let him kiss me," I said, shrugging for emphasis. "My boss was one of the guys *doing me* in the basement. He fired me because I wouldn't kiss him."

Andrew's face pinched in obvious confusion, then he swallowed, his Adam's apple bobbing a few times before he spoke.

"You let him ...," Andrew started, then indicated his meaning with his hand. "And he fired you because you wouldn't kiss him?"

"I know, right? It's totally messed up."

"That's the part that's messed up?" Andrew clasped a

hand over his mouth and started laughing. Which was alright. It was better than the close to vomiting face he'd had earlier.

"Connor …buddy," he said. "You're seriously fucked up, you know that?" He peered down the hallway, but the elevator hadn't arrived yet. "So where does Jake fit into all this?"

"He was the other guy," I replied as I tried to arrange the fridge magnets exactly as I had done earlier in the day before Andrew knocked them all onto the floor. The heavier ones had a tendency to slide, so you had to be sure to start them higher than where you wanted them to end up. That way they would slip into place.

I lifted my finger away and let the last one drift into its spot.

"Is that where you stayed last night?" Andrew asked.

I stepped back to examine my work. All the colorful alphabet magnets Andrew had bought me last Christmas as a joke, lined up perfectly, but I'd spelled out Jake's name with the second set in the midst of all the other patterns.

I hadn't meant to do that. Spell out his name.

"Yeah." I turned away from the fridge as my parents began the long trek down the hallway to our apartment, their arms laden with bags of food.

I headed for the door to help them.

"He took me back to his place," I said, "gave me a bath and put me to bed. When I woke up this morning, he was gone."

That last part made me feel sick. I couldn't understand why Jake had taken off. He'd whispered to me in the basement that we needed to talk, and we definitely needed to, but every time I'd started to say something last night, Jake had pressed a finger to my lips and said, "Not now."

After the bath, I'd passed out, sore but happy, believing I'd wake up in Jake's arms the next morning, but all I'd awoken to was a raging erection and no one to share it with. He better have a damn good explanation for skipping out on me because I'd soaked a small portion of his pillow with my tears this morning, and that had really pissed me off. I hated feeling needy.

Dinner was incredible, especially the steak. My mom knew how to take even the worst cut of meat and turn it into something fabulous, marinating and grilling it to perfection.

I looked up and caught her eye. For some reason, my mom always looked proud of me. I don't know why. I'd never done anything to deserve it.

"How was your dinner, Connor?" my mom asked as she strode toward me to gather up my plate; a plate I knew would soon be replaced by a smaller dessert dish piled high in fruit pie slices and whipped cream. And coffee. There was always coffee.

"Dinner was great, Mom. Thanks for bringing all this food over and doing all the cooking. We were running a bit low on supplies."

"Still no luck on the job front?"

"No." I shook my head. "Not much happening out there. The tourists aren't showing up like they did in previous years."

"Sign of the times, I suppose."

"I guess." I twisted around in my seat. The phone hadn't rung, but someone was knocking at our door. It was likely one of the neighbors wanting to complain about the smoke from our barbecue wafting into their suite. It never failed, but there wasn't much we could do about it.

"Connor," my mom said from the direction of the front entry.

"Yeah, Mom?" I answered, peering at her.

"There's a young man here to see you."

The uncertainty in her voice told me something was up. Full or not, I leapt to my feet and padded across the room to see who was at the door. It was all I could do to keep my mouth from dropping open. Jake's pressed khaki shorts and white, barely buttoned, button-down shirt, were accentuating his sleek body in all the right places.

He looked stunning and gorgeous, and downright edible.

And he was carrying a massive bouquet of flowers.

"Jake? What the fuck?"

"I'm sorry," Jake replied as he fidgeted with the collar of his shirt, which surprised me because Jake didn't strike me as the kind of guy who got nervous …about anything.

"I didn't know you had company," he finished.

I pressed him out into the hall away from my mom and closed the door. "What are you doing here?"

"I wanted to give you these." Jake held up the flowers and indicated I should take them. I wasn't entirely sure I should. If you accepted flowers from a guy, what did that mean exactly?

I stroked the edge of my shirt, then gave in to my impulse and took them.

"Um …thanks," I mumbled, unsure of what to say.

Great.

Now I felt like an idiot standing in the hallway with a bouquet of flowers. I wasn't sure if I should cradle them, dangle them, or throw them over my fucking shoulder.

I was beginning to regret taking them because once Andrew and Karen saw them, they'd never let me forget the day some guy had showed up at the apartment and given their baby brother flowers. I'd never live this one down.

I stroked the smooth edge of one of the petals. My brother and sister could bug me all they liked. I'd never been given flowers before. I was keeping them.

"I'm sorry I took off this morning before you woke up," Jake said. "I had some things to think about. I always think better when I run, so …"

"You went running?"

"Yeah." Jake lowered his gaze. "I know I said I wanted to talk but I kind of …"

"Panicked."

Jake nodded and his neatly combed hair slipped out from behind his ear, descending into a half moon shape that framed his cheek. I almost reached out to tuck it back, but I didn't want to throw Jake off by touching him. He seemed to be on the verge of abandoning whatever he'd come to say and taking off instead.

"Connor, I—"

"Do you want to come inside?"

I know, I shouldn't have interrupted, but Jake was stressing me out with all the stuttering and stammering. I knew whatever he'd come to tell me had taken a lot of thought, and apparently a lot of courage on his part, but I wasn't sure I was ready to hear it.

I clutched the flowers tight against my chest.

"I'd like you to come in," I said, "and meet my family. They're all here for a barbecue. We do it every year. It's kind of a family tradition. My mom makes the best potato salad. I'm sure there's still some left. Oh, and pie. She makes the best pie."

I stopped.

Jake was grinning at me.

"What?" I asked, bringing the flowers up to cover my face. I was blushing profusely. I felt the heat in my cheeks.

"You're beautiful. You know that?"

I blinked and bit into the cello wrapping on the flowers, then peered over the top of them at Jake. I'd never been called beautiful before, and I wasn't entirely sure how I felt about it.

"Connor?"

"Hm …" I lowered the flowers. My mind had wandered.

"I said, I really like you."

I stopped biting at the cello wrap in favor of my bottom lip as I studied Jake's eyes watching me. I released my lip and sucked a drop of spit back into my mouth.

"Are you sure?" I replied finally.

Jake grinned, laughing. "Yeah, I really do, and I don't know if it's too late after what happened at the club last night, but you have to know, I never would've set you up for that if I'd known."

"If you'd known what?"

Jake stepped closer, making me jump a little but in a good way. The guy gave me the most incredible goose bumps whenever he was near me. Whenever he was so close, I could feel his breath dancing across my skin.

My cock throbbed at the thought of him caressing my body with his hands, enveloping my mouth with is, and thrusting into me until my mind filled with the endless points of light he brought to life within me, each one flashing more brilliantly than the rest for a brief moment, over and over again until…

"If you'd known what?" I asked again.

Jake laid a hand on my chest, very near to where my heart was yearning to be released from my body and spoke softly to me. "If I'd known how deeply we connected the day we met. Our feelings for each other nearly knocked me over when you kissed me last night …"

"Jake …," I whispered, in a low breathless tone I hadn't even known I was capable of producing, an unfamiliar sound ripe with longing and something much stronger than desire. I *needed* Jake more than anything I'd ever needed before in my life.

"Connor, I need …"

Oh fuck.

The flowers hit the floor at relatively the same time as my arms found their way around Jake's body, and my lips crushed against his. I was consumed by the moist and furious response I'd dreamt of since I'd woken up this morning without *him*.

"Let's go inside," I said.

Jake dipped down, lifted the flowers, and handed them to me. "We should probably put these in water."

"I'm sure they'd appreciate that." I pushed the door open, flowers in one hand, Jake in the other. This was going to be interesting. Not that anyone in my family would be particularly surprised to find out I was gay, but meeting the guy I was currently sporting a serious boner for, amidst the whole coming out scenario, might be a different story altogether.

I decided to play it casual.

"Mom, Dad, Karen …Andrew," I said as I stepped into the living room, being mindful to keep the flowers low enough to cover the undeterred bulge in my pants from being seen. "This is Jake. I met him last week at the beach, and ah …we've decided to start seeing each other."

"Oh—"

That single exclamation from my dad and a snorting giggle from my sister. That was it. No one else said a word.

"So …we're going to head off to my room," I finished.

"Jake and I still have some things we need to discuss."

"It's nice to meet you all," Jake said while wringing my fingers within his hand. He bumped me through the door of my bedroom faster than I could possibly keep up with, which sent me tripping and landing flat out on my bed. Which was fine by me.

Jake winked at me, unbuttoned his shirt, and landed on top of me. His mouth found mine before I'd even had a chance to ask what his intentions were. I was all for making out in my room, but my family was only one thin wall away from us, and my door wasn't closed.

The feel of his body trapping mine against the bed warmed my balls, and sent tendrils of fiery shimmers into my cock, expanding it past the waistband of my swim shorts…

We needed to stop.

Jake groaned deep into my throat, ran his hands into the small of my back, and down onto my ass. At that very moment, I ceased to care about the world around me.

I pressed my hips up to meet his and tucked my mouth in close to his ear. "Close the door. I need you so bad right now." I thrust up against him, shivering as his hard cock pulsed against mine. "There's no way I can wait until they leave."

Someone tapped on my door.

"Oh, I'm sorry," my mom said as she peered in. "Your door was open. I thought …" She gripped onto the doorframe. "I, oh …"

"I'm going to put these flowers in water," Jake said, then retrieved them and skirted past my mom into the hallway, presumably to the kitchen. I reached for a pillow and held it in my lap as I sat up. My mom didn't need to see the state of arousal Jake had elicited from me.

"Your dad and I are heading home. We'll give Karen a ride, so you don't have to. Your brother's been drinking."

"Thanks, Mom."

She studied me as if contemplating whether or not she wanted to say anything more.

"How long?" she asked finally.

I shrugged. "I met Jake last week."

"No." She clasped her hands together. "I mean, how long have you known?"

How long have I known?

That I like guys?

Was there ever a time I didn't know?

"Mom, I've always known. I just never acted on it. I suppose I should thank Amy for dumping me. I never would've hooked up with Jake if she'd continued to put up with me."

"Things weren't good between the two of you?"

"No, they never were, Mom."

"I thought you and Amy were happy together. You were talking about getting married …"

"Woah, what?" Jake stepped into my room, waited for my mom to say her hushed, rapid goodbyes, then shut the door. "What the fuck, Connor?"

"Jake—"

"Who the hell is Amy?"

I shut my eyes, thinking. There was no easy way around this. Jake had no idea I'd never been with a guy before. That I'd only ever dated girls.

"Had you never …" Jake started, then stopped as he sat on the bed beside me. "But you …" He covered his mouth.

I shook my head. "You were my first, Jake." His expression change from shock to disbelief. Then to something else. The glimmer of something deeper, and it scared me. I wanted it. I knew I wanted it, but it scared the crap out of me.

"Why me?" Jake asked as his palm found its way onto my face. I panted against his wrist, needing him closer. I wanted to taste his skin.

"I just knew." I dampened my lips. "I knew you were the one I'd been waiting for."

"Why didn't you say anything?"

I peered up at him. "Like what?"

"Nothing. It doesn't matter." Jake pushed me over into the untidy waves of disheveled blankets on my bed. They felt stiff and scratchy against my back, but I didn't care. I loved my motley crew of blankets. As a small child, I'd snuggled into them, dreaming of the day a boy meant just for me would find me. Now here he was in these same blankets with me.

I squirmed beneath him, burrowing deeper into the bedding. I needed him. I needed to feel his skin against mine. "Undress me."

Jake slid my shorts off and removed the sheer tank top I'd dared to wear, regardless of what my brother had said about it in the past. Turned out he was right about how gay it was.

I smirked as Jake stripped his clothes off, then surged toward me. He rolled me onto my stomach, then used his tongue to tickle the base of my spine and lick a wet trail up to the tiny hairs at the base of my neck as his cock rocked against my crease, its slippery tip teasing my hole each time it dipped increasingly deeper.

Wait.

I reached back and stopped his assault.

"What's wrong?" Jake asked.

"Nothing." I stroked his ass with my hand. "Jake, I love

when you fuck me, but …I'm also wired to top." I raked my fingers through his hair. "I want …no, I desperately need to fuck you."

"You know I don't do that." He paused for a moment, then climbed off me, and lay flat out on his back. I rolled onto my side, facing him, then remained silent, unsure if I'd upset him.

Jake's chest expanded and retreated a few times, then he looked at me, his eyes rimmed with trepidation. He was trembling. "I've never …"

"Jake, you don't have to—"

"I know, but I think I want to. With you it's different." Jake brushed his hand through my hair. "I trust you and I know you wouldn't ask if it wasn't important to you." He reached for me, directing me to cover his body with mine, then stroked his fingers down the side of my face.

I lowered my forehead onto his. "Jake, if you hate it, I promise, I won't ever ask you to do it again." I set a light kiss on his lips, then Jake flashed me one of his heart-stopping smiles.

So damn beautiful.

I tucked my face against his cheek, then inhaled the tantalizing scent of the taut skin stretching from the curve of his neck to the tender hollow behind his ear. I sucked a lobe into my mouth, savoring it, then ran my tongue along his collarbone to where his shoulder dipped off under his arm. His scent was stronger here, buzzing my senses.

I brushed the bridge of my nose through the soft, fragrant hairs beneath his arm, then spun my tongue in them. My body responded with a shiver that ran straight from my gut to every extremity, and suddenly I couldn't get enough. By the time I dragged myself away, Jake was heaving and struggling beneath me.

He definitely wasn't ticklish, but the attention to the skin beneath his arms, and up and down his throat had left him breathless and his pupils dilated fully, black with desire, tempting me further. I pushed up on my knees and straddled his body.

When he lifted his arms and gripped the pillow behind his head in complete submission, I almost came at the sight of him. He was the sexiest thing I'd ever set my eyes on.

Jake smiled shyly as his gaze drifted down to my cock, then back to my face.

"You want it?" I asked, stroking my cock. It really didn't need the extra attention, it was hot and tight in my hand, but my steady pull and twist had Jake licking his lips.

Jake nodded, reached for my hips, and guided me further up his body. I fell forward, grabbing the headboard and sunk my knees into the pillows on either side of Jake's head.

I gasped at the wet heat as Jake's hot, pink tongue licked the precum streaming from my tip, then he dipped into the slit for more, before sucking me in, enveloping my shaft with his tongue.

My head dropped forward. Jake's mouth felt so incredible, all the time I'd spent edging for my own personal enjoyment was going to come in handy. I didn't want to cum anytime soon.

My stomach clenched, trembling as Jake's hands stroked the back of my thighs, grasped the round peaks of my ass, then pressed my hips forward. The pace he set as I fucked his face almost pushed me over the edge. I pulled back and out and grinned down at him.

"You're way too good at that," I said.

Jake waggled his eyebrows with a bawdy cockiness that was irresistible. I shuffled back down the bed, remaining straddled over his hips, and descended onto his mouth with my own. His lips were moist and soft and still tasted of the strawberry Chapstick I'd seen him tucking into his pocket earlier. I allowed him momentary free reign, and his tongue invaded every possible surface of my mouth until I forced it back. His mouth fell open in response, emitting the most incredible sound.

I echoed it and layered my body atop his, grinding against his rock hard response to our kiss.

"Mm ..." I released his mouth and bit at his chin, pinching and caressing his nipples before slipping down his body to take his cock into my mouth. I played my tongue around the ridge of the crown a few times, then wrapped my hand around Jake's shaft and stretched the skin tight to his body, fully exposing the slick head. As I descended on his cock, it pulsed in my mouth, leaking precum down the back of my throat.

Jake's hand raked through my hair, his hips thrusting. A sound stirred in my chest. The taste of Jake's mounting arousal as it coated the very base of my tongue was incredible. I swallowed and sucked him back to the tip, closing the skin back over the head, and stroked him a few times.

"That feels good," Jake said, then flicked his gaze up to the ceiling. He still looked incredibly nervous.

"Jake, I'll take care of you, alright?"

He nodded, making me feel a little apprehensive. How could I promise him something like that? I'd never done this before.

For him, I can. I'd never hurt him.

I kissed the underside of his cock and licked the crease between his balls, then sucked one into my mouth, savoring its unique taste and texture before popping it back out through my lips. I pressed Jake's thighs up toward his body, and Jake hooked them with his hands. This was definitely new territory for me.

"Fuck." Jake writhed deeper into the bedding.

I'd only touched my tongue to his hole, but it had completely set him off. The tight ring of muscle jumped, pinching closed as I breathed across it. I pried his crease open further and angled in, licking and prodding it into submission.

Jake's hand shot forward and strangled a fistful of my hair, making me release hot exhalations of laughter onto his balls.

"Oh, my God." Jake lifted his head and peered at me. "That feels incredible." He watched me for a second, then lay back down. I smirked and set back at him.

And ...he's never even been rimmed before.

I took the opportunity to torture him a little. Doing so would build up his need, making him less apprehensive. Plus, it made me smile to see him struggling to retain his composure.

When I pressed two fingers inside his ass, stroked his prostate, while sucking him off, Jake truly lost his composure ...and his sense of volume control. I hoped my brother had passed out from the amount of alcohol I'd seen him consuming because otherwise there was no possible way he wouldn't hear Jake's lusty stream of obscenities and cries for me to please fuck him.

"Fuck. Connor. Please." Jake's hands went under my arms and he hauled me up his body, groaning and bucking his hips as he wrapped his legs around me.

I grinned at him. "Are you sure?"

"God, yeah." Jake cupped my face and pressed the most amazing kiss onto my lips. "I want to feel you inside me. I want to feel how much you love me."

I blinked.

There. He'd said it. It was the craziest, most unfathomable thing that had ever happened in my life, and apparently, there was no hiding it from him. I was in love with Jake and he knew it.

I ducked my gaze away and stared at the pillows, almost wishing I could will them into swallowing me up. I don't know why I felt embarrassed, but I did. This was all moving so fast.

"How?" I asked as I stroked the pillowcase behind Jake's head, the heat of his body beneath me reminding me that we were together now. Really together. He wasn't upset with me or feeling like he needed to escape. He'd come to me. Knocked on my door. Wanted into my life.

Regaining my confidence, I met his watchful eyes.

"How did you know?" I asked.

"When you kissed me last night, I felt it. It rocked me to my core. I didn't know what to do with it."

"Hence the running."

Jake nodded and his breathing sped up. He shuddered through a wet gasp. "I've never been in love before."

"Oh, fuck ...Jake." My thumb brushed a tear from Jake's cheek as it streaked toward his ear. He didn't need to say any more. I'd seen it in his eyes earlier. Our hearts had been on a collision course from the first moment we'd met.

Jake exhaled and laughed, smiling at me. I winked at him, kissed his cheek, and rolled away to haul my bedside drawer open. I still had a few condoms left from when Amy used to stay over. No lube though. That was in the drawer of my computer desk.

I scooted off the bed and scrambled toward it, knocking my chair crashing into the wall in the process, which amused Jake to no end. Especially when my brother thumped on the wall and yelled at us to, "shut the fuck up."

Jake was stretched out on his back still creased up laughing when I climbed back onto the bed.

"You're adorable when you're flustered," he said.

"Then expect me to be one hundred percent adorable whenever you're around because you seriously fluster me."

I leaned in and kissed him, then sat back on my haunches between his legs and ripped open the condom wrapper. Jake's hand cruised up and down my thigh, then across my stomach, reaching for my chest and tweaking at my nipples as I organized myself.

I can live with that," he said as he dispensed a sizable dollop of lube into his hand and coated my cock.

He hummed against my lips as I took his mouth.

Um ...yeah. So perfect.

His hand glided effortlessly, twisting and pulling at my shaft, then he shifted, depositing the remainder of the lube into his crease.

His breath shot hot across my chin.

"Could you?" he said, laughing and smiling against my lips. "I can't quite reach." His legs fell open wider than they'd been before and his hips rocked up, causing his ass cheeks to clench as I massaged the lube deep into his hole with the length of my thumb.

"Relax, baby." I brushed a hand across his stomach and he loosened his grip somewhat. "You're alright."

Jake grabbed my arm as I withdrew from his body.

"Be gentle with me, hey?" he said, then dropped his hand to his side. He raised it again to stroke my hip as I hauled his body toward me and caressed his entrance with my cock, preparing him for what was coming next.

I circled his hole a few times, each time pressing

deeper, then held steady and used my fingers to guide the anxious, flushed head of my cock into his body.

His eyes pinched closed.

"Breathe, hun," I said as I slid a little further, then stopped.

Holy fuck.

Was not expecting that.

The feel of Jake's tight ring strangling the head of my cock was unbelievably uncomfortable. I clenched my teeth. My body was screaming at me to thrust fast and hard, and bury my cock inside Jake's body to the hilt.

Don't you dare.

"Fuck, you're tight," I said as I caressed one of Jake's thighs to relax him. Cliché, I know, but he was. I adjusted my grip around my cock and pushed a little further.

"Ah—" Jake's hand slammed onto my chest. "Stop, stop."

"Do you want me to pull out?"

Jake shook his head. "No. Just give me a second." He threw his head back and licked his lips, his shallow inhalations of breath escaping in ragged streams. "Okay, go."

I eased in a bit further and almost lost control when the walls of Jake's ass wrapped around my cock, enveloping it in seductive, pulsing warmth. I fell forward, using one hand placed close to Jake's waist for balance as I caught my breath.

This was more intense than what I'd been expecting.

"You alright there, buddy?" Jake said, ruffling my hair.

Very cute.

I grinned. "I will be in a second."

"Mm …god—" Jake's ass tightened around my cock as I settled my balls against his ass. "Fuck, you're big."

"No, baby …you're big." I backed off and hammered home gently. "I just feel that way in your tight, virgin ass." I filled him again, harder this time, and Jake arched up to meet me. His voice echoed throughout the room with groans and high pitched panting that fired me up each time my cock found its mark deep inside him.

I sunk onto my elbows in order to bring out bodies closer to each other as I continued to deliver each loving thrust, hoping the endless points of light I always experienced when he was moving within me, were lighting up the blackness behind his closed eyes.

Then his eyes fluttered open.

"I'm close," he said as he studied my face, searching for something. "I want to cum with you. Are you able to do that?"

"Mm …hm." I covered Jake's mouth with mine as I increased my assault on his ass, my hips on the verge of cramping as I drove deeper. I released his mouth, allowing the sound that had been building inside him to escape.

"Oh, fuck!" Jake raked his fingers across my shoulders as he fought to keep up with my pace, his own hips rocking against me, drawing me in. "Harder! Oh, fuck! Connor! Harder!"

The air in the room shattered into fragments of rapturous sound, the sheer cresting height of Jake's orgasm beyond anything I'd ever experienced before. It sent me over the edge.

Before the last pulse escaped Jake's writhing body, I dropped my restraint and convulsed into completion, grunting and swearing as I licked the salty, sweat-dampened skin of Jake's throat, and inhaled the musky, seductive scent of my lover.

I came to rest on Jake's lips. His hands swept across

my back, up into my hair, then he ran his fingers through it as our mouths teased each other.

Finally, the fact we were both shaking with laughter had us separating. I landed one final kiss on him. He wrapped his legs around me, sighing and hugging me tight against him.

"I don't know, Jake," I said. "I don't think you liked that."

Jake snorted out a laugh and slapped my ass.

"You were unbelievable," he said, then wiggled his ass around, sending little jolts of overstimulation through my cock and up my spine.

Oh, sweet baby...

It was going to be a long night and would be the first of many days and nights we'd spend together. We'd found *each other* on the beach that day. I didn't know it then, but it was a connection that would last a lifetime, Jake and me.

My Jake.

The boy I'd been waiting for.

The one meant just for me.

Obedience

The tourists were out in full force, soaking in the summer heat by day, and dancing and drinking themselves stupid by night. I was damn lucky they were because it was seriously beefing up my earnings as a bartender back at club *Crush*.

The previous manager Dylan had been fired. One too many times mouthing off at customers.

Jackass.

Served him right after the way he'd treated me. What kind of a guy publicly humiliates you by drenching your fully aroused, naked, shivering body in beer, commands you to crawl across a damp, frigid concrete floor to beg for his thick, engorged cock to be jammed down your throat, spreads your ass and fucks you raw, coats your face in his cum, then fires you.

Reason given.

Insubordination.

Apparently, I'm a disobedient tease because I refused to kiss him. Not that it matters anymore. Dylan's out and I'm back in.

Jackass.

Fucking hot though.

I hummed at the memory of being so thoroughly used in the basement cellar beneath my feet. I'd never done anything like that before. Plenty since, but nothing before.

Not until I'd met Jake.

My hot, gorgeous, and sexy Jake.

Distracted, I pressed my cock against the counter behind the bar to temper my urge to ignore the bubbly, blonde server with the unrealistically perky tits spitting drink orders at me, and seek Jake out in the DJ booth for an extended play, house music blowjob.

God, I love giving him those.

Being forced to my knees beneath the decks of equipment, trapped against his thighs, coaxing every drop from his cock before returning to my post behind the bar, the taste of him salty and familiar on my lips as I poured my next round of drinks.

I grinned against the skin of my forearm, warranting a questioning look from the new manager. I winked at her to alleviate her concerns—and make her blush a little.

She was a sweet girl, but helpless to resist the simplest of my and Jake's charms. Whether or not she believed any of the whispered references to my public display in the cellar was anyone's guess. She never mentioned it and I had no intention of repeating it.

Not here anyway.

My mind wandered again, annoying the hell out of the aforementioned server. The fact I had a job in this town as a bartender *at all* was worth snapping out of it and paying attention.

"Sorry," I murmured, mindlessly mixing the drinks she'd begun punctuating with open palmed smacks to the wet bar top. Despite my outright boredom, I really couldn't afford to lose this job. The economy wasn't turning around as quickly as expected, work was scarce, and I needed to continue pulling my weight at home.

My brother, Andrew, had been concerned about my return to this particular job, but after seeing how close Jake and I had become, combined with a string of promises I'd refrain from ever participating in any further workplace humiliation antics, he'd been more than happy to relieve me of my share of the rent money.

A hot, familiar breath whispered across my ear.

"Hey, sexy."

"Mm …" I responded as Jake slipped a discreet hand into my back pocket, briefly grabbing at my ass before retreating and reaching for a water glass above my head.

"Are you about ready to go?" Jake asked. "I want to be well on our way before sunrise."

"Just say the word."

"Which one," Jake teased as he edged closer, using the confined space behind the bar to *inadvertently* pin me against the sink. It was no secret we were together, but we still needed to watch ourselves. *Crush* was a straight bar. Things happen.

"That you're one hot, sexy bitch," Jake continued, jamming a thigh against the crease of my ass. I sucked in my breath.

Fuck yeah.

Jake's hand traced the back seam of my pants, coming to rest between my legs as he crunched a mouthful of ice in my ear.

"Or that I want to fuck you right here against this bar," he finished, then chuckled in my ear as he released me, leaving me to cling to the edge of the sink and catch my breath.

He had a way of doing that, leaving me breathless.

"Ice," Jake said, snapping my mind away from the image of him bending me over the sink, loosening my belt and hauling my pants down enough to spread my ass and slide his cock into me.

Hot, hard, and fast.

"What?" I asked, peering over my shoulder at him.

No …he would've teased my hole with ice before he fucked me, tracing the pulsing ridge to numb it before pressing the smooth, burning cold into my ass, then he would've made me hold it.

Fuck yeah.

I shivered against the cold, metal sink.

"What do we need ice for?" I asked, half-hopeful.

Mm …the tears would be streaming down my cheeks, wetting my lips. I would've been told to beg for more ice, my legs quivering from the strain before Jake would allow me to expel it.

My legs almost crumpled beneath me.

"For the cooler," Jake replied, laughing. He knew exactly where my mind had gone. "We need to top it up before we head out so the groceries don't go bad," he finished.

"Right," I replied, shaking my head.

Jake and I had mapped out a little excursion, an escape from the mayhem of tourists roaming the streets of our fair city to be more precise, for the only time off we'd likely see all summer.

Jake had suggested camping.

I'd objected, adamantly.

He'd persuaded me using his incredibly talented tongue.

Needless to say, I'm now a camping enthusiast.

The plan was to head toward the Rockies, seek out some secluded wilderness sites to pitch our tent, roast a few marshmallows, fuck each other senseless, and fall asleep beneath the stars. Simple back to basics kind of stuff.

"Do you want me to make you a coffee before we head out?" I asked as I tidied away the rubber mat and shot glasses at my station into the dishwasher, pushing the last of the garnishes down the counter toward the bartender that would be closing up tonight.

I sighed to myself. No coffee for me. I wouldn't need the rousing effects of caffeine because there was no possibility Jake would ever let me drive his baby; a powder blue 1959 GMC Jimmy. It was a beauty, no doubt about that.

Jake had lovingly restored the vintage truck that had been in his family since the day it had been driven off the lot. If it wasn't for the heavy, rubber mats I'd suggested for the box, I'm sure we would've traveled with the camping gear in the cab with us, probably in my lap to protect the seats.

Jake shook his head.

"Nope," he said. "Let's just go."

I threw my bar towel into the laundry on my way to the employee lockers lining the wall near the back door. Jake nipped into the utility room to steal some ice from the spare machine, giving me a few seconds to clear my head.

I was so ready to leave town and have a little down time with Jake. We'd been together for an entire year now and things definitely weren't cooling off between us.

I grinned into the locker and closed the door.

I was so in love with the guy it was pathetic.

"Let's roll," Jake shouted as he jogged past me and threw open the steel exterior door. The stress of the evening drifted away as the cool night air wafted in, drawing me out into the parking lot.

Jake had already finished spreading a new layer of ice in the cooler and was holding my door open for me, making me grin.

Attentive didn't even begin to describe Jake.

He loved me as much as I loved him, maybe more.

When Jake slid into the cab beside me, I reached over, stroked my hand across his face and up into his hair to turn him toward me. I needed a taste of his lips before we set out.

"Always so hungry," Jake whispered, placing his hand on my chest, stopping me and daring me to chase his mouth.

Then his tone changed.

"Say please," he said.

A soft, "please," barely escaped my lips before Jake was on them, his tongue prodding, pushing—overpowering me. A coil of excitement descended from my gut and stirred my cock as Jake's hand crept its way up my chest and around my throat, grasping my jaw and demanding my submission.

Yes. Fuck yes.

I dropped my hands to my sides and relaxed into the seat.

From here on out, Jake would take care of me.

"That's it," Jake said as he pressed my head against the rear of the cab and played with the sensitive lobe of my ear, teasing it into his mouth with his teeth.

A low groan rumbled deep in my chest as I fought to keep from reaching for him, my every breath matching Jake's. He rocked me hard and heavy into the seat, his hand running rough between my thighs, sending my cock thrusting unrequited into the heat dampened folds of my red denim pants.

"Ah—" I gasped, and squirmed as Jake grabbed both my wrists and pinned them to the glass of the window behind me, the hard leather of his bracelet digging into my flesh.

Jake adjusted his grip.

"Tell me what you need," he said.

"I need you to fuck me," I whispered.

"Please," I added.

Jake released my wrists and leaned back in his seat, shoulder to the window, legs relaxed and open, watching me.

"Take your shirt off," he said finally.

The cab was a tight fit even with the bench seating, which I'd hoped I'd be sprawled face down on by now. I managed to remove my shirt without knocking the rear view mirror askew.

Fuck. Jake. No.

I closed my eyes and resisted the urge to object when Jake took my shirt from me and used the pocketknife hanging from his keychain to pierce a few holes in the material before tearing it into strips. It had been one of my favorites.

I swallowed and licked my lips, preparing myself, then turned away from Jake, so he could tie the improvised gag in place. The roll of material was thicker than I'd expected, trapping my tongue, and stretching the edges of my mouth as Jake cinched it tight and knotted it, sending my heart racing as I adjusted.

I inhaled deeply through my nose to calm myself, but the scent of my perspiration after hours of working in a hot and sweaty club, permeated my senses, almost gagging me.

Oh, my god—

My hand shot onto the armrest to steady myself. Jake's fingertips eased my panic as he massaged my shoulders. "You alright?" he asked.

I clenched my eyes shut to trap the tears and nodded my head.

His hands slipped away with a whispered, "Good boy."

The sound of the back door of the club door slamming shut made me jump. The only lights in the parking lot—above the back door of the club ...and directly above our heads.

Jake must've deliberately parked beneath it.

The entire of Jake's cab was well illuminated.

I scanned the lot through my open side window. It was the server who had been annoyingly persistent earlier. She didn't appear to be headed in our direction.

I flicked my gaze back over at Jake, wondering what he had planned for me because he'd obviously planned this.

I didn't have to wonder for long. Jake leaned past me and popped open the glove box. After he finished perusing the contents, I stretched my arms above my head and placed my fingertips against the roof lining. I sucked in a deep breath, holding it as Jake fastened a metal clip to each of my nipples and tightened them. They tugged hot and delicious on my tender flesh.

The chain connecting them came to rest on my chest.

My head lolled back as the euphoria swept in.

Fuck yes.

I caught a glimpse of my reflection, gagged and aching to be dominated. Spikes of pure heat shot straight through to my cock. I struggled to keep my fingers touching the ceiling.

"So fucking hot, baby," Jake said as he moved in, so he could use his tongue to lick slow, wet swaths through the hair beneath my arm, slicking them to my skin.

I shivered as Jake blew across them.

"You like that?" Jake teased.

When I nodded in agreement, he kissed the heat-dampened skin at the nape of my neck and laughed softly as he caressed a hand onto my stomach and swept slow circles across it.

So close.

I bit into the gag as my cock twitched, longing for Jake to continue his attention downward, desperate for the rough haul and tug of his hand. Jake traced a finger up the center of my chest and flicked at each of the nipple clips. The sharp tingle of pain reached my toes.

I met Jake's eyes and blinked, releasing a single droplet of moisture down my cheek. "Tighter?" Jake asked and I nodded.

The increased pinch caused me to flinch momentarily. I sucked in a breath and stole a glance down at the clips.

They were new—serrated teeth with the ability to add weights.

Clamps—not clips.

Fuck.

I squirmed on the seat.

This wasn't going to get any easier.

I needed to remember to breathe.

I braced myself, prepared to maintain my balance as he unhooked my belt and wrenched open the buttons of my pants. They would stay on. They needed to be looser, but they'd stay on for now. We'd played this game before, many times

"You can lower your arms," Jake said, then his lips brushed along the back of my ear, challenging my resolve to remain quiet. A heavy groan of arousal was fighting to escape my body.

I clasped my hands together waiting for my belt to be removed. The extra notches Jake had punched in the thick, black leather made binding my wrists together easy and efficient and secure.

Jake tugged at my cock through the fabric of my briefs as I placed my bound hands on top of my head. His touch was rough, rolling my foreskin back and forth off my cockhead through the material, and hauling on my balls until the ache was almost too much.

I separated my legs a little further to help maintain my balance and give Jake greater access. He shifted in his seat, pulling the elastic of my briefs away from my body. My cock bounced free, the tip glistening wet and slick above the floor mat.

"You'd like some of this, wouldn't you?" Jake asked as he stroked my shaft, slow and steady, then encircled my cock head, collecting a thick stream of my pre-cum on his thumb.

He held it up for me to see.

I would have to beg for it.

"Please," I murmured against the gag, desperate to please him.

My body trembled as Jake smeared my lips in the slick, clear fluid of my desire, painting first the upper one then the lower. He dragged his thumb down the center of my chin and grasped it. My eyes blinked shut instinctively as a wad of Jake's spit hit my cheek.

Jake turned the rear view mirror, so I could see my face. "See how pretty." He stroked an affectionate knuckle along my jaw line. The sound of my heart thundered in my ears. I barely recognized the hazy-eyed, sweat drenched face staring back at me.

I pressed my tongue against the gag and swallowed, then turned my attention out the front window as Jake's hand cupped my balls. He tugged hard on them to remind me I needed to behave, then pulled my briefs back into place.

My mind went blank, focused only on Jake's presence as I stretched my hands forward onto the dash, staring down at the open glovebox in full submission. I wouldn't be permitted to touch him or myself. And if I came …when I came, it would be within the confines of my briefs, and I'd be expected to button up my pants and steep in it.

Please. Jake.

I'm yours—

Please.

My chest heaved as Jake slid two lubed fingers into my ass, jamming my body up against the dash with the initial, forceful thrust. The metal chain tethering my tender nipples to one another swung freely with each aggressive assault, causing the sharp teeth to bite into my flesh.

Jake's hot breath cascaded across the back of my neck as the contents of the glove box shifted beneath Jake's hand. The searing pain shot to my gut from my left nipple first. I had to concentrate, panting into my gag to bring my breathing back under control. Jake's hand came to rest on my stomach, calming me. I breathed easier as the next weight was added to the clamp on my right nipple. I felt the pull all the way through to the skin beneath my arms.

I settled my forehead back against the dash, adjusting my perception to find peace in the swinging pull of the weights.

Mm …there.

Yes.

My cock pulsed, moistening my skin as Jake changed the angle of penetration inside me, manipulating the small gland in my ass beneath his fingertip. I closed my eyes and tipped my hips as he continued to stroke and thrust, rocking my body—building the aching tension in my balls.

Fuck yeah …that's it.

I sucked in a noisy breath past the gag, imagining my lips were wrapped around Jake's thick, gorgeous cock, its slick head stroking the back of my throat as I came.

I peered over at him.

"Not yet, beautiful," Jake said, shaking his head. "I don't want you to cum until I say so."

I nodded, expecting him to continue, but he withdrew his fingers instead. I placed my forehead on my clasped hands and waited.

"Turn around," Jake said finally. "Knees on the seat, looking out the back window."

The sound of the employee door slamming sent my heart racing up into my throat, but I did as I was told. I grasped the back of the seat, being mindful not to sully the dash with my shoes.

I peered out the passenger window toward the club, scanning the parking lot. It was almost closing time. Our well-lit location would soon be flooded with people.

I opted for the view out the back window as Jake hauled on the back of my pants, positioning me so my ass was in full view of anyone walking past the front of his truck.

Fuck—Jake.

He knew exactly how to turn me on.

I steadied myself, ready for what I knew would come next.

The leather paddle came down fast on my ass, sending tiny currents of need straight to my cock. I pressed my forehead to the cool glass and shifted my ass to better position it.

Crack. Another.

Then another.

The front of my briefs were already moist from the penetration, but the repeated smacks to my ass, heating it, released a fresh stream of pre-cum, sticking all the little hairs to the fabric.

The paddle came down again—hard.

I flinched, the alternating strikes becoming more difficult to bear. Jake's intention was clear. He had no intention of fucking me or letting me cum until much later in the evening.

Jake's hand swept soft circles across my ass.

"So pretty," he said. "Hold still."

I sucked in my breath as something slim, cool, and metallic slipped into my ass right up to the hilt of whatever it was. I peered over my shoulder, wanting to see. It took me a second to catch a glimpse of the tire pressure gage in the rear view mirror gliding smoothly in and out of my hole. The sight of it had me squirming, anxious for more. We'd never done this before.

"Slow down," Jake whispered. He caressed a hand down my spine. "Always so hungry."

Jake tossed the pressure gage onto the floor of the cab, then removed a thick handled flashlight from the glove box and set it on the seat beside me.

It rolled into the indent and came to rest against my leg.

No fucking way.

"Breathe, baby," Jake said, then pressed a full set of fingers into my ass. I relaxed, drawing them deep inside until Jake's thumb came to rest on my tailbone.

"Let me hear how much you like this."

Thank you.

Finally.

I pressed my forehead to the back window, groaning with every push and pull of pressure. Filling me, then retreating, Jake's knuckles brushing back and forth across the ring of muscle, once tight, now loose and pliable.

"Fuck, that's it," Jake murmured, angling deeper. My cock pulsed, oozing a deeper stain into my briefs as Jake licked a wet trail along the heated skin of my ass.

Now Jake.

Please let me cum.

I staring blindly out the window, fighting to delay my release as the leather belt binding my hands together rubbed against my cock through the thin fabric of my briefs.

Please now.

Jake's free hand gripped my throat as the other broke free of my ass. "We need to go before the club empties out into the parking lot. We promised your brother."

My gut clenched as an urgent ache ascended from my balls.

No.

I slumped against the seat, almost in tears, after Jake hauled my pants back into place and removed the nipple clamps. I needed to be filled again so desperately, I was shaking.

Three hours out, I was cursing the deficient shock system on Jake's old pickup. Every bump in the road vibrating up through the seat terrified me. Jake had removed my gag temporarily and insisted I finish a couple of bottles of water, stretching my endurance in a direction Jake had never taken me before. His precious seats were being placed at serious risk with every passing minute.

Fuck.

I clenched my ass as Jake changed lanes, running the tires over the rumble strip down the center of the highway. I shook my head to refocus.

I peered over at Jake, at my limit, to plead with him.

A wink was the only response I received from him. A few minutes later, Jake pulled off the highway onto a forestry service access road. I sighed and grunted my appreciation into the moist fabric between my teeth, relief flooding through me.

My door opened, Jake released my seatbelt for me, and I very nearly launched myself past him. Nearly. I knew better than to do that. I remained in the truck.

"Everything off," Jake said, calmly, as if I wasn't about to completely piss myself and soak his beloved leather seats.

Jake ...please.

I leaned my head against the rear window and kicked my shoes off, so Jake could remove what remained of my clothes. The deluge of pre-cum soaking my briefs had dried, resulting in the loss of a few hairs in the process of removing them.

Fuck.

I'd flinched.

Jake smiled, then stroked his thumb down the length of my cock, rousing it from the warm comfort of my balls as my pants were abandoned onto the floorboards at my feet. He lifted my cock and sucked each of my pungent sacs into his mouth.

Jake.

I squirmed and grunted, pleading with my body to concentrate on the sensation of Jake's hot, wet tongue lapping at my balls as he rolled each into his mouth in turn.

I dragged my fingers through his hair, scratching at the top of his head. Jake sighed and ran his hands up either side of my hips and nestled the side of his face in my lap.

God, I love him.

Jake brushed his lips along the skin of my inner thigh, then kissed it.

There was a moment of pure silence as Jake's hands crept around to my ass and gripped my body in a warm, affectionate,—incredibly loving embrace. I never in a million years could've imagined what lay ahead of me, the day I'd met Jake on the beach.

"Right," Jake said, lifting his head. "You probably have to pee."

I tried to smile around my gag, but it came out resembling more of a grimace than a smile. Perhaps it was a grimace. I really needed to go.

I swung my bare feet out through the door and slipped off my seat, landing heavy on the sharp gravel of the forestry road, then followed Jake gingerly to the front of his truck; every step testing the resolve of my bladder.

He stopped and pointed at his truck.

I should've known he wasn't done with me yet.

"I thought we could start our vacation photo album," Jake said as he directed me to back up close to the grill of his truck, legs spread wide, my bound hands behind my head.

I tossed my head to one side, shivering as I positioned myself, the cold air at the higher elevation chilling my skin. I sniffed, wishing I could lick my lips, then stared into the camera, softening my eyes the way I did when Jake's breath caught and he came inside me.

"Perfect," Jake said, followed by the flash of a camera, creating a haze of spots in the darkness, blinding me temporarily.

"Turn around," he said. "Put one foot on the bumper and bend forward a little …"

Oh my god.

Jake, please.

A gust of wind swept down across the road from the craggy rock face lining one side. The hairs on the back of my legs stood on end as I pressed my cock and balls back between my legs, so they'd be visible for the next picture.

The flash lit the surrounding area enough for me to see Jake and I truly were in the middle of nowhere. The trees towering around us on all sides were incredible, their majestic girth and height creating a protected pocket against the world.

My cock swelled warm against my hand at the thought.

No one would be able to hear me out here.

"Let's head off the road here," Jake said from behind me, startling me. My ass pursed tight, tentative as I followed him, a massive flashlight in his one hand, the other potentially ass stretching flashlight from the truck's cab in his back pocket.

I twisted my hands, stretching at the belt, trying to work a little more room between them as I caught sight of a black duffel bag hanging in Jake's other hand.

I knew exactly what was in that bag.

"Put your back against that tree," Jake said.

I complied as quickly as I could. The sooner I did, the sooner I'd be permitted to release the pressure building in my gut. It took me a second to space my feet apart close to the tree but not so close I would lose my balance. The slope banking away from it was pronounced. I stretched my arms up over my head where they would remain until Jake told me otherwise.

The area around us brightened as Jake pulled up on the top of the larger flashlight turning it into a lantern, and set it on the ground beside me. I pinched my eyes shut as Jake sunk to his knees at my feet and placed his hand on my stomach.

He seemed pleased. I'd consumed enough water for his liking.

I spread my legs further apart at Jake's insistence, causing my ass to scrape across the rough bark of the tree. I shook my head, only half-conscious of what was happening around me. The wind picked up. I could tell that much. It brushed past my thighs and teased my cock to attention.

I set my head back against the tree as Jake's hand crept up my thigh, caressing the muscle. He dug his fingers in deep and kissed the underside of my balls, inhaling the scent of the sweat and pre-cum likely still lingering there.

Then he left me and wandered over to a thicket of bushes where he proceeded to relieve himself. He stopped midstream and glanced back at me.

"Don't let me stop you," Jake said. "You really shouldn't drink so much water."

A sprinkling of loose bark peppered my hair as I pressed my hips forward, and released the torrent of piss that had been testing my will. Without the use of my hands, my aim was unpredictable, but I didn't dare lower my arms. I attempted to adjust the angle of my hips by bending my knees a little. The bark gripped at my flesh, reminding me of its presence.

I blinked, releasing tiny rivulets down my cheeks, overcome by the contrasting sensations of pain from the bark, and relief as the last of my bladder emptied onto the ground at my feet.

Jake returned to me and stroked my face. I leaned into it, allowing him to wipe away the tears staining my cheek. I swallowed. My saliva had been building up around my improvised gag, soaking it. A fresh stream of spit escaped the confines of my mouth to grace my chin. It was a particular turn on of Jake's to see my face coated in glistening fluids.

"Beautiful," he whispered, then placed a gentle hand on my back and guided me in the direction of a fallen tree situated a short distance further into the woods. He patted the fuzzy surface of the fallen cedar with his hand, then brushed the loosened moss particles onto his pants. "Do you want a blanket on here?"

I shook my head no.

"Alright, up," Jake said. "On your back, arms over your head, legs draped down the sides."

After complying, I sucked in a cool breath of fresh air as Jake removed the gag from my mouth. He re-secured it further up, covering my eyes, then I heard the crackle of sticks breaking beneath Jake's feet as he walked away from me, then nothing.

Nothing but the wind and the sound of birds beginning their day, until voices and footfalls approached from the direction of the road.

I pursed my lips, checking myself from speaking as a cool, thick-fingered hand caressed its way from my throat, around each nipple and down between my legs, grabbing my balls and tugging hard on them. I took a deep breath, trusting my boyfriend was near, keeping an eye on me. Whoever was hauling at my balls was definitely not Jake.

I opened my eyes and peered down at what little I could see of my chest from beneath the torn remnants of my shirt.

The sun was coming up. Spots of filtered light danced seductively across my skin. It would be a while before the air warmed.

I shut my eyes again as my arms were stretched uncomfortably high above my head and secured. My hips jerked back instinctively as the unfamiliar hand grabbed my cock, and the irritating texture of binding twine tickled the inside of my thigh.

I didn't mind my balls being bound necessarily, but I'd only ever trusted Jake to do it. The rough hands appeared skilled though. I closed my eyes behind my blindfold.

Trust.

It was all about trust.

I exhaled through my mouth and allowed my body to relax fully, pliable and obedient atop the tree beneath me. The tingle started at my lips and descended all the way through my body to my toes. I'd shared with Jake a desire to be used in the forest by strangers.

He'd obviously followed through and arranged it.

"Feet up," I was told but before I was able to comply, it was done for me. Predictably, my ankles were cuffed and attached to a spanner. The weight and clatter of the clips were familiar to me. A sharp tug, as my legs were hoisted closer to my head, followed by the curve of my spine atop the spongey moss beneath me, meant I was now fully trussed, ready to be used.

The tree was low enough to the ground a grown man could easily penetrate me without any more effort than it would require to throw his leg over the fallen tree.

I jumped as a freezing cold shot of lube hit my exposed hole.

"Go ahead," I heard someone whisper.

I replayed the whispered words, searching for something that would assure me I recognized the voice as Jake's, but I wasn't sure. The only thing I was sure of …I was about to be fucked.

My cock pulsed, but what I expected didn't materialize. The object pushed past the anxious clenching ring of muscle in my ass was metal and it was fucking cold. The adjoining arm of what I now realized were industrial sized pliers came to rest on the tight sacs of my bound balls.

The silence around me was fully broken as a round of lust-filled groans erupted.

I counted the voices.

Fuck.

How Jake had managed to organize no less than three men willing to partake in my latest bout of humiliation in the middle of nowhere, I'll never know.

I softened and relaxed as Jake's gentle lips kissed mine.

"You alright?" he asked.

I simply nodded as Jake removed my blindfold, then committed myself to the process as the beast of a man who'd likely been the one handling me earlier, straddled my throat. The coarse, curly abundance of hair covering his balls replaced the memory of Jake's lips against mine.

"Lick em," I was ordered.

Swirling a low hanging, full and sweaty ball into my mouth with my tongue, I coated it in spit, humming as I released it before attacking the other. They went in cool, came out warm and wet. I jerked on my restraints in frustration. I wanted to pack both fat, moist balls into my mouth and gag on them. Be completely smothered by them.

Fuck.

I flinched as the pliers were slipped from my ass, then groaned, which caused the sac between my lips to vibrate. The emptiness was maddening. I let the rigging fully support the weight of my legs, allowing my ass to fall open wider, hopefully tempting someone.

The balls in my mouth were removed, then draped across the bridge of my nose. A string of pre-cum trickled into my hair as the guy above me tapped the underside of his cock into his palm. He caught a thread of thin liquid with his thumb and smeared it across my forehead, then stared down at me, his craggy, weathered face, leering at me, daring me to prove myself.

I nudged at his balls as he separated his thick, sturdy cheeks, then slid my nose along his taint, and tipped my chin up to curl my tongue into the hair protecting his hole.

When I felt the pulsing ridges tighten, I laid swath of spit across the entire surface, then pressed the tip of my tongue inside and settled in, tasting and caressing, making the immense man above me squirm and moan. There was nothing else like it, wielding that much power with something as unassuming as your mouth.

I shifted my hips to accommodate a new burning stretch searing my ass as the trembling conquest above me rocked his hips, forcing my tongue to clean his junk from ass to balls and back again, while he pumped furiously on his cock. I was taken by surprise when he shuffled down toward my chest and released jerking bursts of cum onto my face. The feel of something thick and hard driving up into my gut had blurred my attention.

I opened my mouth, allowing him to feed his drooling, softening cock into it as he leaned forward. He placed his hands above my head and began fucking my face, jamming the spongy tip of the head into the back of my throat. I made the appropriate gagging noises to satisfy him, wanting him off, so I could see what was happening between my legs.

He climbed off and went looking for his pants.

The sight between my legs sent my heart racing.

Jeez, Jake.

The nubby end of Jake's flashlight slipped in and out of my ass, being thrust by a guy about my age. Generationally younger than the one I'd just finished with, but there were definite similarities. He was likely the first guy's son.

I licked my lips. I'd let that guy fuck me in a heartbeat.

They guy cast his gaze downward, scowling.

Shit.

I'd seen that look before.

I lay my head back against the tree and stared up into the canopy above. A dark cloud rolled in and the gentle mist of the first raindrops descended upon my skin. The guy between my feet grunted, disapproving of my relative calm and withdrew the flashlight.

"Fucking queer."

I closed my eyes as a gob of spit hit my cheek. The next one landed on my tongue as he pried my mouth open.

Yeah. Yeah. Just fuck off already.

I struggled against the bindings tethering my arms. Jake was hovering within my sight, ready to step in. I made my decision. I wasn't in to this anymore. Jake had tried to fulfill this fantasy for me, but it wasn't working out the way I'd imagined.

"Red, baby," I said, our safe word for stop.

Jake's response was swift.

"Okay," he shouted as he strode toward me, "he's had enough."

There was a grumbling of disappointment amongst the small group of men, but Jake stepped between me and anyone who might disagree, and within moments of them wandering back to wherever their vehicles were parked, Jake had untied me and lifted me into his arms.

I tucked my face into the warmth of his throat and kissed it as he carried me the short distance to his truck. The emotion bubbling up from my chest as I did so clouded my vision.

I couldn't help myself.

"Don't ever leave me," I whispered.

"Baby, never," Jake said as he pulled open the passenger door and slid me onto the seat. "You're the love of my life." He climbed in and pinned me to the cool leather with the increasingly comforting weight of his body. "I couldn't go a day without your love for me."

I squirmed beneath him.

"I need you to fuck me," I whispered, taking us full circle.

Jake grinned down at me.

"Always so hungry," he said, then unbuckled his belt.

About the Author

Gavin E. Black is the Gay Erotica persona of author, Leigh Jarrett, because every girl needs a naughty alter ego.

Leigh Jarrett is unabashedly queer, quirky, and passionate. Lover of antique stores, the smell of lye and oil as it turns to soap, and the sound of ocean breezes passing through the ancient Douglas firs of Vancouver Island's Cathedral Grove.

In her hometown of Kelowna, BC, Leigh can be found nestled up with her fabulously supportive wife, her trusty laptop, and their persistent treat seeker, Miss Mimi-dog, affectionately nicknamed "Muffin Head."

Having been bullied as a child for being *different*, writing, and publishing LGBTQ Romantic Fiction has given Leigh an opportunity to express her uniqueness, inspired by the LGBTQ community she now calls home. Her contemporary works highlighting their struggles, while celebrating their diversity, and affirming their most basic of human rights—to love and be loved. And her Paranormal and Fantasy works simply sharing the *weird kid* geek residing within her.

Please consider joining Leigh's mailing list:
http://eepurl.com/xuhej

To connect with Leigh Jarrett:
Email: leigh@leighjarrett.com
Website: www.leighjarrett.com
You can also find Leigh on Facebook, Twitter, and Google+